Just a Cowboy's Lifetime Love

Flyboys of Sweet Briar Ranch in North Dakota

Book Eleven

Jessie Gussman

Published By: Jessie Gussman

Contents

Acknowledgments

Cover art by Julia Gussman
Editing by Heather Hayden
Narration by Jay Dyess
Author Services by CE Author Assistant

Listen to a FREE professionally performed and produced audiobook version of this title on Youtube. Search for "Say With Jay" to browse all available FREE Dyess/Gussman audiobooks.

Chapter 1

"I'm sorry for your loss."

Annie Brooks nodded her head, returned the small, perfunctory hug, and swallowed hard.

She had a funeral to get through, and this wasn't the first time, far from it, and would definitely not be the last time those words had been uttered to her that day.

Sunlight glittered down through the fluorescent green of the new maple leaves.

It was her favorite time of year. Late spring tulips bloomed, waving their bright pink and yellow colors, and irises, purple and white, looking stark against their darker green pointed leaves, were planted in clumps all around the large church property.

It wasn't her regular church. She didn't feel at home here. But when planning the funeral, she knew they needed to have a place where they could handle the large inflow of people who would be attending.

She had never seen so many people at a church before.

The parking lot was full, and Ty Henderson was directing traffic to park in the field beside the church. They'd gotten permission from the farmer just in case, and Annie was glad someone had had the foresight to do so.

Cars were backed up on the highway waiting to turn in. They would never all be parked in time for the start of the funeral.

It took her a while to realize that they could delay the start. She was in charge. Technically. She could say she didn't want anything to start until every last car was parked and every last person seated.

The idea gave her something to focus on. Something other than the fact that the funeral she could delay was her husband's.

"I'm sorry for your loss."

Another perfunctory hug, another person with sad eyes, compassion oozing from every pore, squeezed her, then walked away, not knowing what else to say.

She wouldn't know what to say to someone in her position. She honestly didn't know what she wanted to hear. Merle was always the one who had a smile and all the right words. She just stood beside him, complementing him. He could carry the weight of the conversations, the social interactions, give her the bravery she needed to face large crowds of people.

She wished she'd thought to have brought a bottle of water. Her throat was dry; she couldn't swallow.

"I'm sorry for your loss."

Another hug, more perfume, more sorrow, more of her not knowing what to say, and then they walked off.

Lifting her chin, she looked at the large American flag flying between the two uplifted booms of the Mill Creek volunteer fire company. The breeze didn't seem like much, but it put ripples in the flag as it hung suspended high above everyone's heads.

It would make Merle's chest puff out to see it. He always had such pride in his country. And rightfully so. He'd been born with nothing, less than nothing, and he'd become a successful adult.

He'd had the house with a white picket fence, a wife, two small children, and a good job with great benefits.

A dangerous job.

That was the catch, she supposed. There was always a catch.

Two officers, their uniforms crisply pressed, their shoes sparkling in the sunlight, their hats tucked up underneath their arms, walked down past the fire trucks that hoisted the American flag.

The officers' jaws were set, their eyes determined. They weren't expecting to have fun. They were doing their duty. Mourning a friend. Determined to do their best, to pay their respects, to do what they would expect others to do for them if life had gone differently.

"I'm sorry for your loss."

Another hug. More perfume. More uncomfortable silence while Annie tried to figure out what to say. She was sorry for her loss, too.

It wasn't just her loss.

Her eyes tracked across the well-manicured grass to where her mom stood at the swing set, watching her boys play.

Justin, three, understood that Daddy was never coming home.

Times of almost inconsolable crying followed by times of complete normalcy like he hadn't heard that Daddy had been shot by someone who was attempting to rob a convenience store.

The convenience store was safe. The two employees who were on duty at the time were unharmed.

The armed thief was behind bars. For now.

And Merle... He lay in a box in the church behind her. After the pomp and circumstance of today, the lid would be closed forever, and he would be lowered into the hole that was now waiting at the cemetery just a few miles away.

She'd never been to a graveside service.

She wasn't worried about doing anything wrong. Not as much as she was worried about not being able to stop crying.

She didn't want that to be her last memory of her and her husband—her sobbing inconsolably at the edge of the hole in the ground where he would be laid to rest.

She swallowed again, listening to the snapping sound the flag made as the ripples caused by the light breeze shook out. Annie lifted her face to the air that brought the scent of flowers and spring and new birth.

She didn't want to forever associate that smell with sadness and death and devastation.

How could she not? This might not go down as the absolute worst day of her life, the day she found out about Merle would probably have that honor, but this would be a close second.

"I'm sorry for your loss." Another perfunctory hug, more perfume, stronger this time, and it made her dry throat close as she had to swallow the heaving of her stomach.

She tried to smile, tried to look like everything was going to be okay, tried to pretend she wasn't fighting back tears.

Although, everyone would expect her to cry. No one expected her to stand here stoically. She was the only one who couldn't stand the idea of spending the entire day crying.

Crying might be cathartic for some people, but it only made her feel worse.

As though it were possible to feel worse than what she already felt.

A man who looked vaguely familiar strode toward her, and she fought the urge to run away.

Merle had so many friends, from his time in the Air Force, from his time as a volunteer firefighter, and from his job on the police force. She couldn't keep track of all of them. Couldn't keep the names straight. Couldn't remember who he knew from where. Not that anyone expected her to, she just liked to have that information organized neatly in her brain. But it wasn't.

Everyone had told her she was too young to get married. Too young to pledge her life to a man who was a decade older than she. But she had fallen hard for Merle, and he had done the same for her. She thought they could overcome any obstacles life would throw in their path.

And they had. Until last week.

Death wasn't exactly an obstacle to overcome. It was a part of life that one had to walk through. And when that death was one's husband, one had to work through it alone.

Not entirely alone. People wanted to help; she just didn't know how to let them. Didn't know what she needed. Didn't want to be touched or comforted or even to have company. It was all she could do to get her boys up in the morning and get them dressed and try to act and talk to them like life was still going on.

Thankfully, her mother had flown in from her home in Sweet Water, North Dakota. Unfortunately, her mother was trying to talk her into going back out with her. She couldn't. She had the house to take care of, loose ends to figure out, and she already had enough changes in her life. She didn't want to uproot her boys and move across the country. Indiana was a long way from North Dakota.

The man was almost to her now, and no name came into her head. She might have only ever seen a picture of him. Once in a while, Merle would talk about his buddies, show her pictures, and tell her stories.

It had always been obvious to her that the memories he had of his time in the Air Force were good. Of course, Merle loved everything he did; he loved serving as a volunteer firefighter and had loved his job as a police officer, too.

He was in front of her now. The idea that he was from Merle's time in the Air Force tipped in her brain.

"I'm sorry for your loss." The man spoke, his voice holding authority as well as compassion. The kind of voice that had confidence and determination like life was going to go the way he wanted to.

He was much older than she was, Merle's age, but she could disabuse him of the notion. She'd been disabused of it herself recently.

Life didn't go the way a person wanted it to, no matter how hard a person worked for it. God seemed to love pulling the rug out from underneath people so they could fall flat on their faces and wallow in their pain and misery.

"I'm sorry for it too," she said, not sure why those words came out. And now. They sounded bitter and more than a little angry.

The man blinked. He probably wasn't expecting an outburst like that. She presented a picture of youth and innocence, at least that's what she'd been told. She assumed that even though she felt like she lived a lifetime in the last week, she hadn't aged that much.

If the man were religious, he might offer her a platitude about God knowing best.

If he wasn't, he might agree with her that life did suck.

Or he might not say anything, like so many people, and herself, who didn't know what to say.

"If you don't mind, I'll be around tomorrow. I owe Merle something, and I didn't want to give it to you today."

She lifted her chin, hoping that was good enough to let him know that she didn't care what he did. Come around, don't come around. At least he wasn't trying to tell her that God had everything in control. After all, who could believe in a God that would take two little boys' father away from them? Who would allow her world to be upended, after she'd chosen to go against the advice of the world and marry the man she knew the Lord had for her.

He had for her, only to take him away.

Life wasn't fair, and it was really hard to believe that God was good right now.

She thought the man might hug her. Everyone else seemed like they wanted to, but he just looked at her, his eyes searching as though seeing under the surface expression of her face, down into her broken heart and broken spirit. Past the tears she wasn't allowing to fall and into the spot that felt empty and dark, like it would never live again.

"I know Merle had a lot of newer friends, good friends, but I just want you to know that if you need anything, anything at all, you don't have to worry about it, because we will help you."

It wasn't until he said "we" that she realized there were several men standing around behind him.

Funny how she only saw him. She would have sworn he was the only one walking toward her.

Five. Her grief must have affected her vision. That, and the fact that she hadn't eaten for several days. She couldn't get food to slip past the lump in her throat.

"Thanks," she said softly. Happy to hear that the bitterness and anger that had been in her earlier words were not coloring those.

There was some murmuring from the other men around him, then the group strode off, the blond man in the lead.

It wasn't hard to picture Merle walking with a group of men. Talking and laughing. Slapping each other's backs and smiling proudly at his wife and kids. Calling her over, tucking her under his arm, introducing her.

She turned away, not wanting to see the reminder of everything that was wrong. Not wanting to wonder why it was her husband who had died. It was a terrible thought; she had to banish it from her head more than once. Because it kept coming back. Taunting her. She didn't want to be that kind of person. Didn't want to be the kind of person who doubted God the second something terrible happened to her, but how could she not?

She turned, knowing it was time. Time for her to go into the church, sit down at the front of it, beside the coffin, her boys on either side of her, and sit through something she never thought she would, the funeral of her husband.

Chapter 2

Zeke pulled over to the curb, looking at the white house with a white picket fence in front of him. It looked like the quintessential American house. A small yard for the kids to play, a tree with a rope swing hanging from it, a set of monkey bars, and a couple of little toy trucks in a sandbox.

His heart felt heavy, and he remembered the smiling, carefree face of his friend Merle. Merle had been a charmer, always with a date on his arm and always with a backup plan. All the guys teased him about being able to sell insurance or about becoming a preacher. He just had that charisma that made people like him immediately.

It wasn't fake either. Merle had been a good man.

Zeke fingered the money in his pocket. He hadn't known what else to do for the widow, and...he wasn't sure how to get her to take it.

Of course, the easiest thing to do would be to lie about it. Say that he owed Merle money and was just paying it back, or something along those lines. Some people thought lying for good cause was okay, but he just couldn't see that in the Bible. Just couldn't understand how he could justify lying if God said lying lips were an abomination to Him.

Regardless, he hadn't figured anything else out.

Merle had been a good friend to him, loyal and steady, someone he had been confident in, and he appreciated having his support and friendship. Of course, they'd drifted apart after Merle had left the Air Force, but a man didn't walk away from his friends. Or his friends' widows.

She had been younger than he had expected. He hadn't asked her age, of course, but it had surprised him that she looked so fresh faced and innocent.

Barely out of her teens.

Merle and she had had a small wedding, with just family, and Zeke hadn't met her. They'd only been married for a few years. He couldn't remember exactly how long.

Merle left behind two little boys.

Death benefits for fallen police officers were usually pretty good, so Zeke figured she would be fine financially, but the emotional impact of losing one's husband to such a violent death could be difficult.

Regardless, Zeke felt personal responsibility and couldn't leave without giving her something and offering to help if he could.

His buddies had gone back to Sweet Briar Ranch the afternoon before, immediately after the funeral, content to leave him behind to say a few words to the widow and to take care of any responsibilities he might feel like they had.

He took a breath and then walked with as much confidence as he could muster up the front walk and knocked on the pristine white door.

He had his hand raised to knock again before it opened and the woman from yesterday opened it.

"Yes?" she said, her voice young and soft.

"I'm Zeke. I talked to you for a minute yesterday at the funeral. I'm a friend of Merle's."

The woman nodded, her eyes tired, dark circles lining them.

"I...feel a little awkward." He shifted a little uncomfortably, and the woman's mouth moved but not into a smile. She did not ask him to come in. "I have something for you. And I just... Merle was a good friend to me. I know I didn't see him much after you guys got married, so you don't know me. We spent a lot of time together in the Air Force, and I considered him one of my closest friends at one point. He... He was a good man."

"Thank you." The woman didn't say anything more, and Zeke didn't know what to do with his hands, with his feet, with his whole person. It was awkward to just hand someone money, but that's what he was tempted to do. What else was there to say?

"I know if it were me, Merle wouldn't hesitate to help however he could. I would rest easier, knowing that my wife and children would be taken care of because Merle would make sure of it. I... I wanted to give you this." He pulled the money out of his pocket, folded hundred-dollar bills, and handed them to her.

She looked at his hand and then looked back up at him.

He thought she was going to refuse it, because her lips flattened and her eyes looked to the side before she took a breath and then took the money carefully from his hand.

"You don't have to do anything. I feel bad taking your money."

"Please don't. It makes me feel better. I... I wanted to know if there's anything else I can do. Anything that needs to be fixed? Handyman things? I probably can't do a kitchen remodel, but I can patch things together, and I'm a pretty good electrician."

She smiled a little, just a faint smile, one that didn't last long. It made him want to reach out and put his hand on her shoulder, just in comfort. The way a human touch is comforting. But he didn't.

He shoved his hands in his pockets instead.

She shook her head. "I'm going to sell the house. Probably. But there isn't really anything that needs to be done. Just...packing and stuff like that and..." She looked down. "I just haven't been able to think about it just yet. I need a little bit of time to mourn."

"I understand." He'd never lost a spouse, but he understood the need to just allow himself time to get used to the idea of loss. To adjust to a new reality, to figure out one's bearings after their world had been shaken.

She nodded, as though acknowledging that she wasn't the only person in the world who had ever suffered a hardship.

"I'd like to give you my number. Will you call me if you need anything?"

"You can give it to me," she said, but then her eyes narrowed. "Do you live around here?"

He had pulled his phone out, but at her question, he paused, feeling the weight of his phone in his hand, shifting it slightly against his palm.

If he told her the truth, she almost assuredly wouldn't call him. She wasn't going to want to have him run the whole way from North Dakota to Indiana, just to help with the leaky faucet or a light that didn't work in the bedroom. She wouldn't understand that he would be honored to do that. Wouldn't mind at all. Would appreciate the fact that there was something he could do to help his friend. Or his friend's widow, which was the same thing.

"No. I live in North Dakota. But Merle was that good of a friend to me. I'll help you if I can. Just call me."

She looked around, looked away again, blowing more breath out. Her hair was rather dull and lifeless, like she hadn't touched it since she fixed it for the funeral the day before.

It had been a hard day, greeting people, burying her husband, taking care of her children.

"Where are your kids?" he asked, realizing they should have been running around. He didn't have any children, hadn't gotten married, but kids were kind of hard to hide.

"My mom has them."

He nodded, not asking anything else. Like where her mom was or how long she had them for. The woman, he hadn't even gotten her name, didn't seem the most welcoming, and he didn't want to make her uncomfortable by pushing into her personal space.

"She lives in North Dakota too."

He hadn't been expecting her to talk, and her words startled him.

"It's a long way away from Indiana." Her eyes almost smiled. "When she does make it in, she likes to spend time with the kids." She paused. "Thanks for the offer, but I could never ask you to make such a trip." She held up the money. "This was way more than you needed to do. Are you sure?"

"I'm sure. I'd like to do more. And I don't mind the travel. Call me, okay?"

She nodded. "Even if I never call you, it's nice to know there's someone I can use as a backup if I really need to."

If peace of mind was all he could give her, he would certainly do it. She didn't understand that he really meant it when he said that he would come if she needed him. And he wouldn't mind at all.

He stood awkwardly in the door, wanting to say more. Wanting to say a few words about Merle. Wanting to reiterate again that he would not mind doing anything she asked. Wanting to ask how old she was. Which was entirely inappropriate. She looked so young.

"All right. I guess I'll head out. Just take care, okay?"

She nodded, her eyes sad, looking weary as he turned to go.

He thought of her yesterday, her hair swept, her chin lifted, her shoulders back. She faced the funeral and the hard day with courage and fortitude.

It looked like it had cost her.

Wishing there was more he could do, he jerked his head, turned around, and walked away.

Chapter 3

One year later.

This had been a bad decision.

Annie grabbed her suitcase in one hand and the hand of her youngest son Braden, three, in the other and followed her mother up the walk to her house just outside of Sweet Water, North Dakota.

She'd gotten everything settled with her house and job and that type of thing back in Indiana. But there were too many memories in that house for her to be able to stay in it.

The rope swing that Merle had hung, the faucet that he'd fixed four times and had leaked worse every time until finally it was spraying water everywhere. And they'd had to call a real plumber, which they hadn't been able to afford but hadn't had a choice after Merle had "fixed" it.

They'd laughed over it, and Merle had gotten a job delivering pizza on his days off in order to pay for it.

She'd been pregnant with Braden, and Justin had been less than a year old.

She'd missed her husband but appreciated the fact that he took care of her.

She always felt cared for with Merle.

The last year had been hard. And she wondered over and over again whether the people who had said that she was too young to get married had been right.

She hadn't thought, still didn't really think, that she had been too young. She didn't regret that at all, but she was too young to be a widow. Too young to have two boys to raise on her own. Too young to have any idea of what she should do with the rest of her life looming ahead of her and their boys depending on her and she had no idea what to do.

She'd ended up moving back in with her mother.

It felt like she was moving backward in her life, not forward. But she didn't feel like she had a choice.

"This is Grandma's house?" Braden asked, looking around with wide eyes. Braden and Justin had been the only two reasons she had been getting out of bed for the last year.

It honestly wasn't even that she missed her husband so much, although there was still a painful hole where her heart used to be.

She wasn't quite sure what it was. Just a general lethargy about life.

Her counselor had said she was depressed, but she didn't want to believe that, and she had eventually quit going.

She hadn't realized how far in debt Merle had been. He had started two businesses that had failed before he became a police officer, and he also had several large credit cards maxed out which she hadn't known about.

All that stuff had been before they had gotten married, and she didn't blame Merle for not wanting to tell her.

Regardless, it made the money that she had received from his death disappear quickly.

"Am I gonna get my very own bedroom?" Justin asked, and Annie nodded. That had been something Justin had been looking forward to, although she wondered how long it would last. Her boys had shared a room since they'd been born, and she suspected that Justin wouldn't enjoy his own room quite as much as he thought he was going to.

Still, her mother's house had four bedrooms, and for the time being, they were going to be using all of them.

For the time being, maybe forever. Who knew? Annie didn't have any other plans, other than to endure life until it was over. Raise her kids. Do her best with that, but everything else just felt so hopeless.

Maybe the counselor was right. Maybe she was depressed.

"All right, the movers arrived yesterday, and they put all of your beds together, and so your rooms are all set up. I'll show you up the stairs." Annie's mom grabbed Justin's hand, sharing an excited smile with him.

At least her mom was happy to have them move in. Or she seemed that way anyway. As an accountant, her mom made a good living, and now that tax season was over, it was the perfect time for them to move in.

Her mom could have made the decision a lot more difficult by acting like it was an imposition, but she seemed thrilled to have her daughter back underneath her roof.

Her dad had died shortly after she got married, and her mom had lived alone all of that time, flying back to Indiana to visit as often as she could, which was usually once or twice a year.

She led them up the stairs and showed each of the boys their rooms, which included all of the things they'd had in Indiana, plus a few new special toys that Grandma had provided.

The new toys caught her boys' eyes immediately, and Annie had to admit she appreciated it. After the two-day drive across the country, she was ready to sit down and take a little break. And while she loved her children, sometimes their constant demands were exhausting. Particularly when she was driving. Children were not meant to be raised by a single mom.

A husband would have helped a great deal to take some of the load off her shoulders.

Lord, I miss him.

She hadn't continued to blame the Lord for Merle's death, and most of the time, she didn't even question it anymore. Even if she still didn't think it was fair.

But she supposed she still had the nagging feeling that God didn't really love her. If He did, why did He let something so terrible happen to her?

After finding out about all the debt her husband had accumulated, debt she hadn't known about, her opinion of him had shifted. Of course she still loved him, but she realized there was a lot about him that she hadn't known.

"Let's go downstairs. The boys will be fine here, and they'll know where we are if they need us," her mom invited her, but it was more of a command.

Her mom had been on her because she hadn't jumped right back into life like her mom thought she should. It was perfectly normal for a person to sit around in their PJs all day, drinking soda and eating chocolate chip cookies. Everyone had days like that. And when a person lost her husband, they had more days like that than a normal person did.

Surely her mother understood that.

Her mother led her into the kitchen, and she went to the cupboards, looking for coffee mugs to put on the table while her mother heated water and got tea bags out.

"I have a couple of job offers lined up for you. I've been asking around town, and it's a small town, so everyone knows you're arriving. You'll need about a week or so to acclimate, and then—"

Panic bubbled up.

"Mom. I'm going to need more than a week."

"Honey. It's far past time you got a job."

Annie pressed her lips together, shoved the fear back down, and got two spoons out of the drawer.

Her mom was right. She hadn't worked for over a year. And she needed to. The funds had disappeared, and while she had sold her house and that had netted her a little bit of extra, it wouldn't last long.

She didn't want to work. She didn't want to do anything. She didn't even want to get out of bed. The only reason she did was because of her children. And now that her mom could watch them, she had looked forward to being able to sleep as much as she wanted to. Which was pretty much all the time.

"Now, Sweet Briar Ranch outside of town is hiring. They started a dude ranch, and they need someone to help with booking. Those skills are right up your alley, and I told him that you'd be out for an interview later this week."

"Mom. I just need some time." She didn't feel the slightest bit ready to go out and start talking to people. To work. To be expected to function like a normal human being.

It felt like way too much for her to handle. It was enough just trying to keep up with the boys.

"I'll still have a little bit of work to do now that tax season is over, but I can do that in the evening and I can watch the boys during the day."

"I wanted to be able to stay home and raise them."

It was funny, wasn't it? Her whole desire had been to be a stay-at-home mom. She'd never dreamed of doing anything else. And how many women were there that felt like they were stuck at home, or stuck with kids, and had zero interest in being a mom? It just didn't seem fair. The things that a person wanted, someone else got, while she got what someone else wanted.

"We've been over that. You need to get out." Her mom, serious for once, the smile off her face, looked over her glasses and met Annie's eyes. "You had a year. For your children's sake, you need to get back out."

She pressed her lips together and sat down at the table as her mom poured steaming water into her mug.

Her mom filled up her own cup before she put the water back on the stove and sat down at the table.

"You can waitress at the diner. That job's open. It would probably be more evenings and weekends, which would give you the days free. They're also looking for a secretary at the church. And there are several other ranches in the area who might be hiring. Plus, the Olympic Training Center is looking for an activities director for their off hours when they allow the public access to their facilities. That would be a job where you would have a lot of contact with people. I know you're more of an introvert, and I didn't figure you'd probably be interested in that one, but I wanted to mention it."

Annie sat still, listening to her mom as she continued to ramble on, talking about the pros and cons of all the jobs she had lined up for Annie to apply for.

Annie had zero interest in any of them. But she had no other plans for her life that she could use as an excuse to decline her mom's well-intentioned intervention.

If she had been able to stay in Indiana, she probably should have done so.

"All right. You guys have the rest of the day to acclimate. Church starts at eleven tomorrow. Sunday school's at ten. We can walk down the street when it's nice. It's a few blocks, but it's a pretty walk."

"I haven't been going to church," she said.

Her mom's face fell, and Annie felt bad for disappointing her, but if she was going to have to get out and get a job, that was one thing, but she definitely wasn't ready to go back to church. At least with a job, people weren't going to be overly nosy, but at a church, people wanted to know your whole life story, and they wanted to butt in and help wherever they could.

She didn't want help. She just wanted to be left alone.

"If you're living here, you're going to church."

Her mother didn't raise her voice, but she said it in the tone that she'd used all throughout Annie's childhood when she meant what she said and what she said was not to be argued with.

Annie closed her mouth and looked away. She would be going to church in the morning.

That evening, after Annie had put the kids to bed, and her mother had retired to her room, she walked down the stairs, unlocked the front door, and went outside, sitting down on the steps. She wrapped the blanket that she'd brought with her tight around her. She'd talked to her mom enough over the years since her parents had moved to know that North Dakota didn't warm up as quickly as the rest of the country, and sure enough, the night was chilly.

Something moved in the darkness as Annie settled down on the step, and she froze.

Was there some kind of wild animal roaming the streets?

But as the shape drew nearer, it filled out into a cow form, and Annie laughed at herself. Cows were benign, even one with horns as long as this one had. It looked a little shaggy too, a little like a prehistoric mammoth. Except, it wasn't nearly that big.

Her mom had told her about the steer that roamed the streets of Sweet Water.

She wished her boys were out, because they would enjoy seeing it.

Expecting the steer to continue walking by, Annie was surprised when he slowed. He must have smelled her or something, because he turned toward the steps where she was sitting and lifted his head, taking a few deep breaths with his nose and blowing it on Annie, fanning her hair away from her face.

The smell was not unpleasant, and Annie smiled.

That action felt odd. Smiling. She hadn't done much of it over the last year.

"You lost?" she asked.

Maybe it was the sound of her voice, or maybe it was his intention all along, but the steer moved toward her, his long horns waving as he took a few steps, until he stopped, his nose resting softly on her knee.

Annie was too surprised to move, and then, as the animal just stood there, one of her hands came out from underneath her blanket, and she patted the wide forehead before scratching between his ears.

That seemed to be what the steer wanted, and he slowly rolled his head from side to side, his wide eyes closing in enjoyment.

Billy. That was what her mom had said the name of the steer that roamed Sweet Water was. He looked like a Billy. And she hummed a little as she continued to scratch.

Somehow, petting the steer was soothing, and she relaxed, not even really realizing that she had been tense. The move, the pressure from her mom to get a job, her children depending on her, and her fear that she wouldn't be able to raise them alone had been harder on her than what she realized. She felt it all draining away.

Maybe, maybe she had been looking at it all wrong. Maybe this new step in her life wasn't a backward step. Maybe it was the beginning of a beautiful new future. She just had to have the courage, the energy, the desire to start moving forward.

Chapter 4

Zeke parked his pickup in the church lot and got out.

Miller, the only other unmarried man on Sweet Briar Ranch, got out from the passenger side.

All the other flyboys who had started the ranch with them now had their own families and went to church with them.

Not that Zeke minded; he had no intention of getting married. It was good for other people, but he just wasn't the kind of man a woman wanted to settle down with. He wasn't sure exactly how he'd come to that conclusion or what made him that way, but it was fine by him. He had a nice routine and didn't really care to have it interrupted the way a wife would most definitely interrupt it.

"Hey, Smith's over there. I wanted to ask him how his family back home is doing. I'll be back, but you can go on in without me," Miller called across the hood of the truck as he looked down the parking lot at Smith who had just parked his SUV and was helping his family out.

Zeke lifted a hand in acknowledgment and turned toward the church.

He stopped short as he saw a familiar figure with a small child on either side of her walking with Bonnie Fox.

Merle's wife.

He never had learned her name. It might have been over a year since he'd seen her last, but he felt like he'd recognize her anywhere.

His heart hurt.

The last time he'd seen her, she looked exhausted, tired, and grieving.

She didn't look quite as grief-stricken, but she still looked tired and haggard. Like she hadn't been taking care of herself.

He swallowed, thinking about Merle and how he would be sad to see his wife had been struggling in the year since he passed.

One of the boys stopped on the sidewalk, pulling his mom's hand until she stopped and looked down at him.

He pointed over toward a tree and chattered about something, although Zeke was too far away to hear what he was saying.

As he went closer, he could see the mom shake her head and tug a little on her son's hand.

"Maybe after church we'll have time to go over and see, but not now."

"It's a squirrel nest, Mom!" he said, peering over again, like he was going to miss the only time in his life that he would ever get to see a squirrel nest if they went to church at that moment.

"We don't have time. We need to figure out where your classes are, and then we'll have to make sure we know where we can meet after Sunday school."

"I can help you with that, ma'am," Zeke said, watching as her mom disappeared into the church holding the taller boy's hand.

The lady's head jerked up, and her eyes widened before they narrowed like she was trying to place him.

Obviously, she didn't remember him. And rightfully so. She'd probably seen hundreds of men on the day of her husband's funeral.

It was the biggest funeral he'd ever been to.

"I'm Zeke. A friend of your husband's. I saw you at his funeral and the day after."

"Oh. That's right. Zeke." She smiled, a small smile, and held out her hand, clasping his.

"I don't think I ever got your name," he said, unsure how to ask for it but wanting to know it.

"Annie. I'm sorry. I'm Annie."

"I never thought I'd see you here in Sweet Water."

"You live here?" she asked, her brows coming down, like her brain was sluggish and catching up, as though it hadn't thought to wonder what in the world he would be doing here in North Dakota of all places.

"I do. My buddies and I own the Sweet Briar dude ranch that's just outside of town. Your mom had inquired about positions that were open, but I hadn't realized that she was your mom. I guess I should have."

"No. There would be no reason for you to do that. Her last name is different, of course." Her son tugged on her hand, and she gave Zeke an apologetic look before she looked down.

"Mom. I think it's a squirrel nest."

"I can show you to your classes. I'm one of the hall monitors and know more about Sunday school than a man with no children probably should."

She smiled a little bit at that too, but just one of her soft, small smiles that was gone within a few seconds of crossing her face.

He'd like to see her with a big smile or a full-on laugh. She probably had a beautiful laugh. Merle loved to laugh, and he could just imagine this woman smiling at his friend and laughing at his jokes.

"Oh. Okay," she said, looking back down at her son. "This is Braden, and he's three. And he loves squirrels. All animals really, but squirrels seem to be a special favorite." She lifted her shoulder like she wasn't quite sure how he'd gotten attached to squirrels but he had.

"I don't think that's a squirrel nest you're looking at, but we can go over and check it out if you want to," Zeke offered.

It was for Merle. This woman still looked tired and grief-stricken. He wanted to help her somehow, now that she was in Sweet Water, and apparently looking for a job, because she hadn't denied it. She was basically in his backyard. And he could help.

They walked over, the little boy trotting beside him. He looked down at Braden.

"So you're three?"

Braden nodded, his head going up and down, his chin bouncing off his chest with each nod.

"Wow. That's pretty old. But you know what, we would only need one digit for both your age and my age."

"Digit?"

He should have known a kid that age would not understand the word "digit." He hadn't been around too many little kids.

"It's a number. You're three. And I'm thirty-three. And all we need to write our ages are threes."

"You're the same age as Merle."

"I thought we were about the same," he said, answering Annie's whispered words.

"I'm twenty-three. So to write all three of our ages, we just need two digits. A two and a three."

He'd thought she was young. Although, she looked a lot older this year than she had last. It had probably been a tough year for her. That made him sad. To think of her trying to handle everything alone. Although, that was probably a misconception. She likely had plenty of people helping her.

They reached the tree, and Braden pointed up to the small hole he had seen from across the yard.

"I can't quite see it, but I can lift you up and you can peek in," Zeke offered.

Braden nodded his head eagerly and let go of his mom's hand immediately, turning fully to Zeke and holding his arms out.

"Let's get you turned around so you're facing out. I'll set you on my shoulders, then see if I can grip your legs to hold you up."

"Be careful," Annie said softly.

He jerked his head at her but didn't say anything. Like he would do something dangerous with someone else's child. Someone he just met. A widow.

But he didn't express his consternation that she would even think such a thing.

Lifting Braden up, he settled him on his shoulders and then, grabbing a hold of both of his legs, carefully and slowly lifted him as high as he could.

Braden could just see in.

"It's empty," Braden said, disappointment oozing out of his voice.

"It might not always be empty. Maybe we just caught it on a bad day. Maybe a bird usually lays her eggs in there or something."

"Do you think?" Braden asked, hope entering his eyes again as Zeke set him back down on the ground.

"It's possible. That's what animals often do, they find a hole like that in a tree and turn it into a good place to raise a family."

"Like squirrels!" Braden said, smiling up at him.

They continued to chatter about animals and nests and squirrels as Braden easily took his hand and they started walking back toward the church. Annie walked along with them while they headed toward the three- and four-year-old Sunday school classroom.

"After Sunday school, the teachers of the younger kids lead their children directly to junior church. You can take him upstairs to the service to be with you if you want to, or you can meet him after church there, which is the entrance to the junior church room." He pointed to the last door down the hall.

"Oh. So I wouldn't need to come get him after Sunday school?" Annie asked in surprise.

"No. They usually have the older kids in the service for the beginning, then they let them go. But the little guys don't do that."

She nodded and then looked at her son. "Is that all right? Did you hear what Mr. Zeke said? I'll see you after junior church?"

"All right, Mom. You be good," Braden said, grinning at her, like he knew that's what she always told him, and so he was beating her to it.

She smiled, kissed him on the forehead, and then straightened.

"It's not hard to get back to the steps to go upstairs, but I can show you," Zeke offered as they watched Braden walk boldly into the group of kids.

"All right. I think I know, but I guess if we're both going the same direction, you might as well."

He didn't remind her that today was his Sunday to be hall monitor and he wouldn't be staying in the service.

"Are you here in Sweet Water to stay?" he asked with what he hoped was casual interest as they started walking.

"Yes. For now anyway."

"I see."

And then, words he hadn't considered until just then popped out of his mouth. "Would you like to go get ice cream after church?"

He wasn't sure why he asked, and so he felt like he needed to explain. "Not as a date or anything. Just because you're the wife of one of my friends, as a welcome-to-town thing."

She smiled, one of those small smiles again, and shook her head. "You don't need to do that. I'm going to be just fine. I mean, it's going to take a little getting used to, but that's life, right?"

"Yeah. It is. If you need anything, I don't want to be pushy, but just call. Do you still have my number?"

She nodded. "I'm sure I do. I put it in my phone. And...what was your name again?"

He laughed at himself, although he didn't allow the smile to come out on his face. "Zeke."

He'd not made a big impression on her, that was for sure. But it wasn't that he was trying to be romantic, he was just trying to be helpful. It was obvious that she had been struggling for the last year, and having just moved into town, she probably didn't have a whole lot of friends who would get her out of her house and involve her in activities. That's probably what she needed. That's what he thought anyway, although he certainly wasn't any expert in grief and depression, but she just seemed...more sad than anything. Or tired. Maybe both.

And it stirred his heart and made him want to help.

"All right. Here are the stairs; they'll take you right up to the sanctuary."

"You're not coming?"

"No. I'm the bouncer today." He grinned a little at his joke, but she looked at him in confusion.

"I walk around, making sure that no one who doesn't belong here is here. Churches are kind of sitting ducks for people who have wrong intentions. And with all of the anti-church rhetoric, I suppose it's important to be careful."

A cloud passed over her eyes as he spoke, and he kicked himself.

Her husband had been a policeman. She knew exactly what he was doing. And he had reminded her of what her husband did.

Of course, he hadn't thought about it that way. Not until he saw the expression on her face. He hadn't meant to upset her.

"I'm sorry. I forgot about Merle."

She shook her head. "It's okay. You can't go walking on eggshells around me, scared you're going to say something that's going to upset me."

"Well, people don't like to upset other people. At least I don't."

"It's me. I need to...get over it."

"Maybe you can...get out a little. That would probably help you get over it."

"Maybe I can figure out how to get over it on my own, thank you anyway," she said, surprising him with the irritation in her voice. "Thank you for showing me the door." She spun, not exactly grabbing the handle and yanking the door open, but showing more fire than she'd shown the entire time he'd known her, all of ten minutes.

He grinned a little after she left. At least the fire was better than the sad, melancholy ghost of a girl who she had been before she got angry.

Normally, he didn't laugh at people who were angry, but her anger made him smile. It was a better emotion, in his opinion anyway, than what she had had before.

She had turned him down, but he didn't take the rejection personally. Didn't take her anger personally. She obviously was still hurting. He didn't want to be a pain, but he'd keep his eyes open for a way to help.

Chapter 5

"I heard that you were talking to Zeke Butler at church today. Why didn't you tell me that?"

The kids were upstairs taking a nap, and Annie sat at the table, chopping strawberries for a salad.

She wanted to take a nap herself, but she felt like she needed to do something in order to earn her keep. Her mother wasn't charging her rent, although she could have, and Annie didn't want it to be said that she was taking advantage of her.

Still, she certainly didn't feel like sitting at the table working. And she definitely didn't want to be grilled by her mom about some man who was only being nice to her because of pity because he was a friend of her husband's.

"I'm sorry. I didn't realize you'd want to know. Plus, I couldn't remember his name."

It was true she'd forgotten it, but she remembered it now, although she hadn't known his last name.

"He's a nice guy." Her mom's statement didn't exactly hold a question, but it was obvious that her mom wanted to know the details.

She supposed it would be better to tell her that she'd turned down Zeke's offer of ice cream than to tell her that she turned down Kenni and Eliza's request to help them make soup on Tuesday for shut-ins, and that she also turned down Malley and Darby's request for her to visit the nursing home on Wednesday.

She also turned down a request from an older woman to help with the spring festival. She'd wanted her to man a booth or something.

She felt like the folks at church had...not attacked her, exactly, but had wanted for her to feel included so much that they made her almost feel accosted instead.

Zeke had been the first of those invitations, and she didn't regret turning him down. She didn't want someone to be spending time with her because of pity.

She wasn't lonely anyway. She just wanted to sleep. And wallow in her misery. She didn't understand why people wouldn't just let her wallow.

"Annie. You can't spend the rest of your life sitting around at home, feeling bad for yourself. It will be good for your kids to have some friends. And it would be good for you to have some friends who are men."

"I don't want men friends." She wasn't interested in any kind of relationship. She wasn't going to go so far as to say that Merle was the love of her life and she would never marry again, but...it just felt so hard. Dating, deciding whether or not she liked someone well enough to spend the rest of her life with him, constantly wondering if she would be able to handle any bad habits he had. Wondering if he would be able to handle hers. Whether he'd love her children, whether he'd take care of her, whether he was going to be the kind of man who cheated.

Exhausting.

"I'm not even talking about romance," her mom said defensively. "I'm talking about...the human need for companionship. For someone to talk to. To spend time with. To get out and see some of the town with someone else. Another human being."

"You don't have someone like that," Annie pointed out, then regretted it. Her mom seemed happy, and she didn't want to destroy that.

"I have plenty of people. I don't have a significant other, true, but I was married to your father a little longer than you were married to Merle."

"That doesn't make any difference, Mom. And I haven't been on you to try to find someone else to replace Dad."

"I'm not asking you to replace Merle. I was just telling you not to close yourself off—"

"I'm not closing myself off. I'm just uninterested."

"Isn't that the same thing?"

"No."

She was being a little bit harder on her mom than she should, and she knew it. It made her feel bad. But at the same time, she twisted the strawberry in her hand, not knowing how to explain how she felt. She didn't know. She just wasn't interested. Didn't want the problems that a relationship always brought, didn't want to expend the energy.

Although, if she was being completely honest with herself, Zeke was a nice person.

Her mom's shoulders slumped, and she looked at her with regret.

"I'm sorry, Mom. I'm sorry." She sighed. "Zeke's a really nice person. He was friends with Merle. But that's just it, he sees me as Merle's widow. He feels bad and pities me. Thinks I need...help or something. He's not being nice to me because he likes me. He's being nice because he liked Merle."

"What does it matter? Why are you digging into his motivations? You assume you know what they are. Maybe you don't."

"All right. Say he asked me for ice cream because he likes me. He's...a nice guy. Steady. But look at him compared to Merle. I mean, Merle was laughing, happy, friends with everyone. He made me laugh all the time. We had such a great time together. I... I could always depend on him to keep me...not happy exactly but looking at the world through the rose-colored glasses that you need in order to not see all the depressing things around you. Merle just did that for me. But Zeke, he's so serious. I mean, I think I've seen him smile, but it's not the same, you know?"

"So you talked to him for a while?" Her mom pounced on the little bit of information.

"No. Ten minutes tops. But I did see him at the funeral, and he came after the funeral and gave me money."

That made her mom's eyes widen, and the look of interest intensified.

Annie wished she wouldn't have told her. She actually hadn't even used the money. She'd tucked it away, and she didn't want to think it was an idol, or that she was using it as a sense of security rather than depending on the Lord, but it was just nice to know that she had money tucked away. That if something happened, she wouldn't be completely destitute. She hadn't needed to use it, and she was happy about that, but it had been just a nice little bit of reassurance in the back of her mind.

Someday, someday when she felt better, when she didn't feel like life was so hard or so hopeless, she would thank Zeke for the money. Not because she needed it so desperately, but because it had been one of the few small things that had comforted her over the past year.

"Merle was a great guy. You know I loved him like he was my own son. I thought he was a great father to your children, and he was an excellent husband to you." Her mom's hand came over and covered hers. "But he's gone." Her words hung in the air.

Annie determined that she was not going to cry. She wasn't still desperately in love with her husband. She didn't even desperately want him back, although she did in a way. Want him back.

Wished that he hadn't been killed, of course, but it wasn't that she was still hung up on him. Not really.

"You have to be able to move on. You aren't living. You're just existing." Her mom's eyes were tortured. Sad, and there was a little bit of fear in them too. Annie hated that she made her mom feel that way.

She also knew that her mom was right. She wasn't really living.

"I'm just not ready."

"You're out here now, that is a step in the right direction, but you can't just sit around here at the house. You have to get up and do things." Her mom's lips pressed together. "You don't have to work. I'm making enough money through my accounting business that we can live here comfortably. But getting out and doing something would make you feel better. Just try. Please?"

Her mom had opened up her home when Annie hadn't had anywhere to go. Her mom had taken her children and watched them as much as she possibly could, giving Annie time to grieve. Even before that, she came out and watched the children so that Annie and Merle could go away together.

Her mom had been the very best mom and grandma that she could possibly be.

Annie knew she owed her. But this seemed like a steep price to pay.

Still, she hated the worry and concern and fear that was in her mom's eyes.

"I'll try." She could promise that much. She just didn't know whether she would succeed or not. But as long as it wasn't necessary for her to actually be successful, she could at least try.

"All right. Thank you. I appreciate you saying that. I know that if you say you'll do it, that means you will."

"But, Mom?" Annie said, turning her hand so that it clasped her mother's.

"Yes?" her mother asked.

"Please stop pushing me. I promise, I will try to get out. I'll try to do whatever it is that you want me to do. But I feel like people are constantly pushing me to do what I'm not ready for. And it almost takes as much energy to struggle against that as it does to actually get out and do anything. Do you understand what I'm saying?"

"But you believe me when I say that I'm only doing what I think is best for you? Sometimes we have to be uncomfortable in order for us to feel better. In other words, sometimes things get harder before they can get better."

She couldn't argue with her mom. That was true. When a person was sick, sometimes they had to take medicine that didn't taste very good in order to get better. Or just when a person didn't think things could get any worse, they got worse, but then eventually they got better. She supposed even when exercising, a person felt like they were going to die and they couldn't breathe, and they hurt the next day, but in order to get in shape, it had to happen.

She supposed her life was the exact same way.

Lord, give me the strength and courage to do the things I don't want to do.

Chapter 6

"I now pronounce you man and wife," the preacher said, looking at Miss Agnes and Mr. Marshall. "You may kiss your bride."

Mr. Marshall turned, but before he could bend down, Miss Agnes reached out, grabbed his cheeks, and slapped a big kiss right on his lips.

There were slurping sounds that made Toni's stomach turn just a little, but Mr. Marshall seemed to be having a good time, so she figured it was okay.

Thankful that her parents hadn't felt the need to be quite so noisy anytime they'd kissed, Toni averted her eyes, and looked over at Sorrell and Merritt.

They were both smiling huge smiles, standing between their mom and their new stepdad, who had a baby in his arms.

Their mom was just starting to show, and her baby bump was adorable.

Toni leaned into her own mom, her own baby bump was just slightly larger than her friends' mom's.

She was going to be a big sister, and she couldn't wait to get started.

She didn't care if her parents had her babysitting every day, in fact she hoped they would. She wanted to dress the baby and change her and bathe her and get up in the middle of the night and feed it bottles and teach it to walk and talk and ride bikes and swim and she had a million things she wanted to do with her baby brother or sister.

Her parents had decided to be surprised, so they hadn't found out the gender.

Everyone laughed as the kiss ended, and Miss Agnes grabbed Marshall's hand and held it in the air.

"If y'all want to come, we're taking a trip across the country on our mopeds!" she exclaimed, leading Marshall down the aisle between the rows of congregants.

Everyone cheered, and Toni turned to watch as they disappeared out the front of the church.

Turning back to the altar, she saw Mr. Blaze and Mr. Junior standing there, looking a little forlorn.

That gave Toni an idea, and she slipped through the crowd, going around the edge as people filed out of the church, tapping Sorrell and Merritt on the shoulders.

"Guys," she whispered, waiting until they turned around, then filed out of their pew, and followed her toward the front of the church, away from everyone who were gathering around to wish Miss Agnes and Mr. Marshall a safe journey.

"What do you think if we try to match up Mr. Blaze and Mr. Junior?" she asked, tilting her head and raising her eyes, excited at the direction her thoughts had taken.

Sorrell and Merritt didn't respond for just a moment, then Merritt smiled.

"That's brilliant! They helped us. I mean, they tried to anyway. And you know that they are going to be lonely now that Mr. Marshall isn't going to be around anymore. Maybe we can find someone..."

"Maybe we can use TikTok?" Toni suggested.

"Or we can make a new recipe. Not Marry Me Chicken, maybe Marry Me Beef?"

"Maybe. We can experiment with it anyway."

That's a great idea. I mean, we can get Billy into the act, too," Merritt said.

"Billy, Miss Charlene, Miss April, everyone! If we all start working on it, surely we'll find someone."

"Be careful, because if we go too far, they're going to start thinking that there's something wrong with them that we have to have the whole town involved in finding someone for them."

"Better that, and happily matched, than having their feelings hurt."

"We can do it without hurting their feelings. We just have to figure something out." Toni bit her lip. The church had emptied out quickly, so the girls hurried outside in time to see two mopeds buzzing down the street, Miss Agnes's orange and green hair waving in the wind.

Toni, busy trying to think of a way to introduce Mr. Blaze and Mr. Junior to their lifetime loves, was startled when she almost ran into a giant black dog.

"Oh!" she said, stopping abruptly.

Sorrell must have been in as deep a contemplation as what she was, since she ran into her back.

"Oh!" Sorrell said.

Thankfully Merritt stopped without running into anyone, and they faced the large, black dog who seemed friendly.

"It's a pretty dog, ma'am," Toni said, a little embarrassed to have almost run into the lady and her dog.

"Her name's Georgie," the lady said with a smile.

"Can we pet her?" Sorrell asked, and Toni wanted to shush her. They shouldn't ask strangers if they could pet their dogs.

This lady was obviously a tourist, since Toni knew everyone in town and this lady was not from Sweet Water.

"Hey, Georgie," Toni said, patting the dog's head.

"You girls haven't seen an older lady walking around anywhere, have you?" The man who stood beside the woman holding the dog asked.

"I've seen a lot of older ladies today, but I don't know if I've seen the one you're talking about," Merritt said, stepping forward and holding out her hand. "I'm Merritt, and these are my friends Toni and Sorrell.

"I'm Jeanette, and this is my husband Dave."

"Are you looking for someone who lives in Sweet Water?" Merritt asked, and Toni admired how confident she sounded. Maybe someday she'd be able to talk to strangers that way.

The lady had a little bit of an odd accent, which made Toni think that maybe she wasn't even from the United States.

"We are. Although, we're from South Africa. But, we had heard about the Marry Me Chicken, and we decided we weren't getting any younger and we would come check it out. Georgie usually stays with friends, and she loves that, but we thought she might enjoy North Dakota as well."

Toni thought flying with the dog might be pretty hard, but she didn't ask them how they did it. Sometimes it was easier to just not know, and accept the fact that it happened.

"So do you like it here?" Merritt asked.

"Very nice. But, we had a friend with us. She was originally from North Dakota, and she was going to show us around. But, we've lost her."

Just then, they heard laughter, and they all turned to look in the direction of where the sound came from.

Mr. Blaze was standing and talking to a woman who was about half as high as he was, and she had blue hair.

"Nevermind. I just found her. Looks like she's found someone to hang out with," Dave said.

Georgie barked, just one bark, but Toni kind of thought that maybe Georgie was giving her stamp of approval.

"I think we might have lost our guide," Jeanette said with a laugh.

"My friends and I were just trying to figure out how we could find someone who would be perfect for Mr. Blaze. Maybe we're not going to need to do anything after all," Toni ventured into the conversation.

"I didn't even know Marie was looking for romance," Dave said.

"I think if a woman is single, she's always looking. Sometimes we're just a little picky," Jeanette said with a small laugh.

Georgie seemed to agree, because she tilted her head, and whined just a little.

"Do you girls have a suggestion of where we should eat supper?" Dave asked, obviously having his fill of romance, and interested in the more entertaining pursuit of filling his stomach.

"My parents own the diner, and it's the best place in town to eat," Merritt said, and she didn't even sound conceited when she said it. Just matter-of-fact.

"I have to agree. Her mom really knows how to cook."

"They allow dogs too, especially if you sit at the tables they have sitting on the sidewalk. They do that in the summer," Sorrell added, giving Georgie's head another pet.

"All right. We'll take your word for it. The locals always know the best places, don't they Dave?" Jeanette asked, the man nodded his head.

They look like a couple who had been married forever, happy together, and almost to the point where they read each other's minds.

Toni wasn't sure whether she would ever be married that long or not, but she wanted to be. She wanted to have a marriage that lasted all of her life. Just like these people with the pretty black dog.

Chapter 7

"How are things coming out on the new dude ranch?" Harry Rismore asked as he packaged up the screws and staples Zeke had purchased.

"Doing good. We have our schedule open for summer, and people are booking. Which kind of surprises me, but that's what I hear anyway."

"You're going to have real-life people hanging out at your dude ranch this summer?" Harry said.

Zeke laughed, causing several other customers to look their way. "That's exactly how I feel about it. It's pretty unbelievable."

"That old farm sat there for years, with no one showing any interest in it at all, then you guys come around, and all of a sudden, everything is happening." Harry shook his head. "I can't say I don't like it. Business has been booming for the last few years. And I only see it getting better if we're bringing more people into town."

"There are positives and negatives with that, but mostly around town I hear the positives," he said. It was true, some people didn't want their small-town way of life to change. But most people were happy for the increased business and acknowledged that most of the tourists who came into town were considerate and kind.

"What's the special at the diner today?" Zeke asked as Harry handed over the small, heavy bag. Baker and Kenni were the only ones at the house this evening, since Miller was out on a crop-dusting run.

Zeke liked to give Baker and Kenni as much privacy as he could, and while he didn't find it awkward to sit with them, he did feel like they probably appreciated having some evenings where Baker's friends weren't hanging around interrupting their privacy. They were planning on building a house, but they hadn't started it yet. Zeke didn't mind sharing a house, and he didn't think that Baker and Kenni minded. Still, it was kind to give them a little bit of time away.

"Meatloaf and scalloped potatoes."

"That sounds good enough to eat." Zeke grinned.

"I can tell you it was good at lunchtime today," Harry said.

"Think I'll check it out. Thanks for these." He held up the bag. "I'll be seeing you around."

Harry nodded, and Zeke walked out the door, the bell ringing as he went out.

He walked to his pickup and put the screws and staples on the seat, then shut the door and let the pickup sit. It wasn't far to the diner, and he figured he'd just walk down. It was a nice evening, chilly, but with a slight breeze, which was normal for Sweet Water.

He'd been serious about what he said to Harry. Excited about the ranch and the future.

But he felt a little restless too. That wasn't something that he talked about to too many people, because he didn't want his buddies to think that he was going to ditch them and go running off somewhere.

He didn't have any plans like that, but he just felt unsettled in a way that he hadn't for a long time. Not since he was in his early twenties.

Part of him thought it might have something to do with Annie. Seeing her in town, wanting to help her, and being shut down.

She probably thought he wanted to help her because she was his buddy's widow. Which, if he examined his motives too closely, was not entirely true.

He couldn't deny that he had approached her to begin with because of Merle, but there was something about her. Maybe it was the way she looked tragic and sad. Or maybe it was the way he just felt an instinct telling him she needed help. He wasn't sure, but she'd been on his mind, and he did the only thing he could do. He prayed for her.

He was still walking toward the diner when Billy came out from between two buildings, startling him out of his thoughts.

"Hey there, bud." He stopped a minute to scratch the steer between his ears and wished he had some treats to give him.

The town seemed to take care of Billy pretty well, and Zeke wasn't concerned about him being hungry. It was just fun to feed him.

"Zeke Butler. Just the man I was hoping to see."

Zeke looked up to see Miss April coming out of the diner and hurrying toward him.

"I'm just standing here waiting on you, ma'am," he said, giving her his best charming smile.

He wasn't exactly known as a flirt or schmoozer, but he looked at Miss April with affection. She meant well anyway.

"I'm looking for people to sign up for the spring festival. And I hope that you'd be able to take a turn in the dunking booth."

Zeke laughed. "Did you go down through your list trying to find the biggest suckers, and my name came up?"

Miss April almost looked affronted. "Why no. Of course not."

But she didn't offer any explanation as to how she figured that he would be good at the dunking booth.

"Is there something else you'd rather do?" she asked, holding out the clipboard that held a bunch of papers that rippled slightly in the breeze.

"The dunking booth is fine. I suppose it would be too much to ask to have it on a day that is ninety degrees and lots of sunshine?"

"The spring festival is usually about forty degrees and sometimes we even get wet snow flurries," Miss April said, pushing her glasses up her nose and looking at him over the top of them.

"Yeah, that's about what I figured. Sign me up for the dunking booth. It's been a while since I've had a good round of pneumonia."

"That's the spirit," Miss April said approvingly, nodding and scribbling on her clipboard. She didn't waste any time getting his name down. "And I'm looking for someone else to man a wheelbarrow for the wheelbarrow race. We're getting a bunch of different people to help out."

"All right. You can sign me up for that too. Probably after I'm done in the dunking booth so I can get warm."

"Oh, I'm sorry. It'll be before. The dunking booth can cool you off." Miss April put his name down again and then looked up. "I'll make sure your times are in the schedule I hand out." She hooked her pen on the clipboard. "I'll see you at church on Sunday. And I'll have everything you need then."

"All right. Sounds good. When is this thing again?"

"It's Monday. Memorial Day."

"All right. I'll be there." Zeke couldn't add that he was looking forward to it. That would have been too big of a lie. But he understood the responsibilities of living in a small town. Sometimes a person had to go along with wild and crazy schemes, because when he had a wild and crazy scheme, they'd go along with it in return.

Like starting a dude ranch with his buddies.

Plus, he wasn't too big on relationships and all that jazz, but it really did foster a sense of community. He wanted to be a part of that. After all, the small town had welcomed him with open arms. And he would give back if he could.

Miss April said a few more words and then strolled on down the street looking for her next victim.

Zeke shoved the uncharitable thought out of his mind. He really didn't mind helping.

As he turned to start walking back up the street, he saw Bonnie Fox, Annie's mom, and her two grandsons holding onto each of her hands.

Annie was not with them.

He strode forward, meeting her at the diner door and opening it for her.

"Good evening, ma'am," he said as he held the door.

"It's a nice one," Bonnie said, and her smile was genuine, although there was worry in her eyes. It wasn't hard to see.

"Is Annie okay?" he asked the only thing he could think of.

One side of Bonnie's lip flattened and pulled back.

"She just doesn't seem to have any interest in life. I can't seem to get her to want to do anything." Her voice was pitched low, and she tilted her head as the boys let go of her hands and ran into the diner.

He understood that Bonnie wouldn't want the boys worrying about their mom. It was hard enough that they'd lost their dad and moved across the country.

"She's not sick, just...depressed?"

"She insists she's not. I begged her to go to see a counselor, but she claimed the last one she saw wasn't doing any good and made things worse." Worry lay heavy in Bonnie's eyes. "I'm not sure what to do."

"Do you want me to see if she wants to come eat?"

He didn't know what else to offer. It wasn't like he had any experience in depression or anything of that sort. Of course, he'd seen men in the Air Force struggle. In his experience, the best thing they could do was to force themselves to get out of whatever hole they were in and get busy doing something. Once a person took their eyes off themselves, they got so busy helping others they forgot to be sad.

He wasn't so naïve as to think that was a cure that worked for everyone, though.

But Annie didn't seem to be deeply depressed or even suicidal. Just sad. Just having trouble getting out of the rut of thinking about how her life didn't turn out the way she wanted it to.

"I'd appreciate it. Different people have tried. Everyone at the church has been so friendly. But she's just...hard to reach."

He nodded, figuring that if she wouldn't go to a counselor, she probably wouldn't take any medication. He wasn't a big fan of it himself, but he understood that sometimes it was necessary.

When one of his buddies in the Air Force had gone through a bit of a downtime, he'd seen different articles that said that most depression could be cured by changing the way a person thought.

The problem was, it was up to that person to change the way they thought, and while in the depression, that was hard.

"I just need to warn you, she's probably not going to be receptive to anything you suggest."

"I kind of figured. I feel like I'm bugging her, but..." He didn't know what else to say. He wanted to give the excuse that she was Merle's widow, but that really wasn't it. Maybe at first, but there was definitely something about Annie that haunted him.

"Hey, Grandma! Are you coming in?"

"I need to go," Bonnie said, giving him a smile that still did not mask the worry in her eyes.

He nodded, holding the door until she walked in and then allowing it to slide shut. He said a small prayer before he started walking up the sidewalk that the Lord would give him the words to say. Help him to know what to do, to switch Annie's brain, and help her see that there was so much worth living for.

It didn't take long to walk to Bonnie's house, and to his surprise, Billy was already there.

"Hey, buddy, I still don't have any treats. But it's good to see you again," he said as he scratched the steer for a few seconds before he walked up the front porch and rapped sharply on the door.

He figured if he were timid or a little bit unsure, Annie would just turn him down flat. He needed to have confidence and be...not pushy maybe, but determined.

He waited for what seemed like a long time before he rapped again.

It still seemed to take a long time before there were clicks as the lock was turned, and then the door opened.

"You," she said as a greeting.

"Good evening. It's nice to see you again as well."

She seemed to almost roll her eyes, flattening her lips and turning her head.

He laughed, because it was obvious she was fighting herself. "It's okay. You don't have to be nice to me if you don't want to."

"I thought I was going to have a quiet evening by myself, and now you."

"I know. I'm a pain. I saw your mom as I was going to the diner, and she said she's worried about you. I told her I'd run up and see if you want to come down and eat with us."

"I already told her no. Did she tell you that?"

"She did. I just figured I'd ask again. I... I can see she's worried."

"She doesn't need to be."

All he could see was her head poking around the door. Her hair seemed dull and unbrushed, and the dark circles that he'd noticed under her eyes on Sunday were still prominent.

"She's your mom. I think that gives her the right to worry if she wants to."

He didn't want to argue with her. Didn't want to be antagonistic toward her. That wasn't the way to win an argument and to get her to come out.

"Would you like to sit on the porch with me?" he asked, figuring that he had a better chance of getting her to come on the porch than of getting her to go down to the diner.

"I'm not really dressed for it," she said, sounding tired and lethargic.

"I'll wait while you change."

She sighed and looked toward the wall. "If I sit on the porch for five minutes, will you let me go back inside and not harass me about going to the diner to eat?"

"Sure. I wasn't planning on harassing you anyway. Although, you're right, I was gonna see if you wanted to go eat with me."

"I already told you. I understand you were friends with Merle, but you don't have to look after me just because you have some kind of buddy pledge or whatever you guys do." She shook her head, and that time, she did roll her eyes.

"Maybe I didn't tell you, but it is really not because of Merle. I've been thinking about you a lot, and Merle certainly hasn't figured into those thoughts at all."

He hadn't really meant to say that, but it was true. Hopefully she read it as him being a concerned friend and nothing more. Because there was a little something more. He wasn't sure exactly what, but it wasn't just because he was concerned about someone new in town. There was just something about Annie that pulled at him. Made him want to get closer, and made him care. It was a natural caring that he didn't have to put on just because she happened to be the widow of his friend.

She pressed her lips together even harder, and he thought she was going to turn him down.

Then she said, "Fine. I'll go put something on that I can be seen in and sit with you for five minutes on the porch. Then you can go back and tell my mom you got me out of the house. Deal?"

"Sure," he said easily, waiting until she backed away and shut the door before he walked over to one of the posts beside the steps, leaning his shoulder against it and shoving his hands in his pockets.

Why was he even here?

Just because he couldn't quit thinking about her didn't mean that he needed to butt his nose into her business.

But somehow he'd ended up here without even really intending it. He thought he'd run to the diner, grab some supper, give his friend a little privacy with his wife, and then head home. Maybe work out in the barn a little before bed.

Certainly hadn't planned to spend his evening here, sitting on the front porch swing with a woman who didn't want to have anything to do with him, but one he couldn't seem to get out of his head.

As a Christian, not necessarily as a man, he knew he needed to care about her.

But this wasn't something that was forced. It was something that...he seemed to do without even thinking about it.

He watched Billy contentedly chewing his cud on the sidewalk right in front of the house, thinking to himself the next time he came to town he needed to make sure he brought some treats or something for him.

It was a good ten minutes before he heard the door clicking again and the screech of hinges as it opened.

"You're still here."

He huffed out a breath and looked over his shoulder. "Did you think I was going to leave just because you took a little while?" He certainly wasn't going to be put off that easily.

"Maybe I hoped."

That was a little hurtful, and he tried to remember that she wasn't feeling well. She didn't mean to be mean, and she didn't mean that little dig in his heart.

The door pushed open, and she stepped out. She'd put on jeans and a T-shirt. Her feet were bare, but she'd brushed her hair.

"I think you're going to be cold."

"I'm not planning on staying out long," she said easily, giving him a smile that said she knew she was going to be cold, and she also knew that he wasn't going to force her to stay outside when she was freezing.

"Fair enough," he said, pulling his sweatshirt over his head and walking over to the porch swing.

She sat down on one end, and he sat down on the other end with plenty of room between them.

"Then we'll be cold together," he said as he put his sweatshirt on the seat between them.

Her lips pursed, and she looked at him, then she looked away, her arms crossed over her chest.

"You don't have to be cold just for me," she muttered.

"It would make you feel better if you put that on, and then when I get cold, we'll quit. That way, you don't have to suffer."

"I'm already suffering by coming out here. I might as well be cold too."

"All right. We might as well dress for the weather we wish we had, rather than the weather we do."

She tilted her head at him, then huffed out a surprised laugh. "Positive thinking?" She laughed again. "Does that work for you?"

He touched the tip of his finger to his tongue and held it up as though taking the temperature of the air. "Not yet."

She huffed out another breath, and he felt like that was a win. At least she was smiling and didn't seem to be perpetually annoyed with him.

She pursed her lips and turned her head, looking straight ahead. He got the feeling she was trying not to enjoy his company. He hoped that was the case.

Chapter 8

Annie tightened her arms against her chest and tried not to shiver.

It was freezing out, and she really should have brought a sweatshirt.

She could put Zeke's on.

She didn't want to touch it. Didn't want to capitulate. Didn't want him to know that she wouldn't mind staying out just a little longer. He was funny. She hadn't realized. Merle had always been able to make her laugh. That had been one of the best things about him. Zeke seemed so quiet and almost taciturn in comparison.

But there was a dependability in Zeke that Merle hadn't had.

She hadn't realized how bad it was until after he passed away and she'd realized how much debt she had to deal with.

Zeke seemed like the kind of man who was responsible, but she wouldn't have guessed he had a sense of humor too.

Still, she had to admit it felt good to get out of the house. She hadn't left it for several days, using the weather as an excuse, but it really wasn't that. She just...didn't feel like doing anything.

"So you want to tell me why that steer always seems to be hanging around your house?" Zeke asked in a casual tone that didn't seem contrived, although if he had been relegated to talking about a cow as a conversation starter, he was really grasping at straws. "It seems to be here every time I drive through town."

"So you notice my house?" she asked, trying to make him uncomfortable. She couldn't help but think he was just there because of his friendship with Merle. But if she kept pushing him, making him think that she thought he was there for romance, maybe she could drive him away.

He seemed like the kind of man who would be easily embarrassed about that type of thing.

Not that she was an expert at manipulating things to embarrass people.

Before she became a widow, she used to be a nice person.

She wanted to be a nice person again, she just didn't feel happy.

Happiness is a choice.

She heard that a million times before. She supposed she believed it, but maybe she just didn't want to choose to be happy. She just enjoyed wallowing in her misery.

"I don't know. He's supposed to be a matchmaking steer. Maybe you better be careful, you might end up being married to someone who is grumpy and mean."

"I actually have some buddies who swear by the steer. That he really is a matchmaker. That's how they ended up married." Zeke's words seemed thoughtful, and he moved, one hand reaching up and hooking onto the chain on the porch swing, the other resting easily on his leg.

He didn't seem cold. Unfortunately.

"I don't hold any credence to that. Not for me anyway. I was married once, and I'm certainly not interested in doing that again."

"Merle was a good husband," Zeke said casually.

"He was. But that abrupt ending was pretty hard."

To say the least. She hadn't been expecting it, even though she knew his work was dangerous. After all, the odds were still far in her favor that he would come home every night.

"Just because something is hard doesn't mean we quit," Zeke said, though his words held no heat.

"When your wife dies, you can lecture me. Until then, you really don't know."

"I guess that'll be hard, since I don't have a wife." He grinned a little. "I wouldn't be sitting here on the porch swing with you if I did."

She glanced at him, then looked away. He refused to take offense. Even when he certainly had a right to. She hadn't been very kind.

"Well, that's good to know. If I were your wife, I wouldn't appreciate you sitting on someone else's porch swing, even if it was the widow of an old Air Force buddy."

He moved the swing slightly with his foot, not quite enough to rock back and forth, but enough to give it a little gentle movement.

She didn't say anything more, and somehow the night felt almost peaceful. She didn't quite feel content, but other than the cold, she almost felt...okay.

"Has Miss April been around to sucker you into doing something for the spring festival?" he asked, after a few minutes of gentle breeze, gentle swaying, and gentle silence.

She was almost disappointed that he spoke.

"No. Or maybe she has. I don't know." She really couldn't remember. "I think someone asked me to do a few things. I had a bunch of different people come up to me in church on Sunday and ask me to do things. I don't remember what or who." She didn't really care either. She could barely muster up the energy to get out of bed; she certainly couldn't take on any other responsibilities.

"You'll be busy taking your kids around anyway."

"I wasn't planning on going."

"Your boys would love it."

"Maybe Mom will take them."

"I bet you anything the ladies have your mom roped into helping in the kitchen. They always sell a ton of food at those events, and it takes a small army of people working to make that food and serve it."

"You sound like an old hand. But you can't be a Sweet Water native."

"No. You're right. I moved here after I got out of the Air Force. I bet Merle would have come with us if he hadn't been so stuck on you."

"Maybe." Indiana had been Merle's home, and that's where he had wanted to settle. Annie hadn't cared. She was just happy he was finally out and they could make a life together outside of the military.

"I ran into Miss April on the street by the diner just an hour ago, and somehow she got me signed up for the dunking booth. So, if I'm annoying you right now, you can plot revenge."

She found her lips curving up, completely against her will. What was it about him? He wasn't Merle, with his overstated humor, but he just had a fun, gentle way of teasing her that made her laugh.

Made her want to smile, it was breaking down her walls, and that made her very uncomfortable.

Not so uncomfortable that she wanted to leave him. She actually wanted to scoot closer. Or at the very least, pick up his sweatshirt and put it on.

"All right. Noted. I love the dunking booth, and I will be there with bells on."

"You better be careful, Miss April might sign you up for it too."

"I'm not afraid to tell Miss April no."

He laughed. "Are you calling me a pushover?"

"I bet you're not used to that, are you?"

"I guess I'm probably not." He lifted his shoulder. "Although, Sweet Water has been good to me, good to my friends. I probably would do pretty much anything anybody asked me to do. Especially if it's something that makes the town better. After all, I want other people to feel as welcomed and at home as what I do."

That was a good way of looking at it. She liked a man who wasn't afraid to give back. Who didn't feel like he needed to take all the time. Merle could be selfish. Quite selfish. It was one of the things that bothered her about him, but she always reasoned with herself that no one was perfect.

And he provided a good home, made her feel happy and secure, gave her a full sense of security.

"I suppose that was a hint that I should give back too? After all, I'm landing in Sweet Water here, with my life in shambles."

"What happened to you was tragic. And you're right. Sweet Water is a great place to land and put things back together. I'm sure that you're going to do it."

"I don't know. It just seems so hard."

She didn't mean to confess that to him, but it wasn't like she was telling him something that he didn't already know.

"Maybe that's because you want to look at the big picture. Just focus on little steps. You know, coming out to the porch and sitting on the porch swing until your nose freezes. Baby steps like that."

"All right. I'll sacrifice my nose for a baby step."

"That's the spirit."

This time, they both laughed softly together. And she reached for his sweatshirt.

"Is the offer to wear this still on the table?"

"Sure is." He wasn't gloating, and he didn't even let a satisfied smile cross his face. And she appreciated it. After all, it took a certain shoving aside of her pride to admit that she wanted to stay, which was essentially what she was doing when she said she wanted to wear it.

She put it on. It was still warm from his body, and his scent clung to it.

She supposed she hadn't recognized that scent from church, but it was unique. Different than Merle, of course. But not unpleasant.

The sweatshirt hung on her, but it felt comfortable, and she snuggled down.

"I'm sorry I was mean," she finally said.

"You weren't mean. You just didn't want to be bothered. Then I was pushing you a little harder than you wanted to be pushed."

"You're not even going to let me apologize?"

"If one is necessary, I'll accept it. That one wasn't."

"Maybe it would make me feel better."

"All right. I accept. You're forgiven."

"Aren't you going to make me work for it?" He was too easygoing and agreeable. She wanted an argument.

"Hardly. I didn't think you owed it to me in the first place. But if you feel guilty, just throw money."

She snorted. "Like I have any money to throw around."

"Merle should have had a pretty good life insurance. Not that it's any of my business."

"He did. But it just barely covered his debts."

"Ah. I guess I probably knew he had debts. But seems like when someone passes away, you forget all the bad things, and you just kind of idolize them in your head."

"That's fine. I don't want to talk bad about him. But I didn't want you to think I was independently wealthy. If you're after me for my money, you're better off finding someone else."

"That changes things."

She laughed, assuming he was joking since he was laughing too. "You don't have to agree with everything I say."

"Hey, if you start throwing money, it won't be hard to get me to agree to pretty much anything."

"I don't believe that."

"No, but it sounded good."

"I suppose."

His stomach growled.

"You really haven't eaten?" she asked, remembering that he said he had seen her mom heading into the diner.

"No. I told your mom I'd come up here and see if you wanted to come eat, and I guess I kind of forgot about it."

"It sounds like your stomach is reminding you."

"You interested in coming?"

"I think you pretty much convinced me that you really are just trying to look out for me. But...not really."

"Is it going to bother you if I don't give up on you?"

"No. I... I think it's going to make me feel like someone cares."

"Good. Then I won't give up on you."

"Here. You can have your sweatshirt back."

"No. You keep it. Maybe you want to stay out here a little bit longer. I'm going to head out. You're not wrong, I am starving. Breakfast wore off a while ago, and I realized I forgot to eat lunch."

"So I'm not the only one who forgets to eat sometimes?"

"Guess not. Although I don't forget often."

He stood, and she stood with him. "If my kids don't remind me that they're hungry, sometimes I wouldn't eat all day."

"That's not really a good thing. You're too skinny. I know, that was personal, but it's true."

"I think if you told me I was too fat, that would be a problem. But I'm not going to get offended if someone's going to tell me I'm too skinny."

"All right. I won't take it back."

"Zeke?" she asked as they walked slowly to the steps, where Billy stood at the bottom, his head over the last two steps, munching contentedly on his cud.

"Yeah?"

"Thanks for caring. I do appreciate it. Even though I know it probably seemed like I didn't."

"I think that there's a lot of people who care about you."

"But you've been the most persistent."

"I'm not sure that's a compliment but...thanks."

"It was a compliment." There was something about him, something about his calm, funny, compassionate demeanor that made her feel like he really did care.

"All right. I'll see you around. And... I won't give up on you."

"Thanks. Good night, Zeke."

She didn't mean to, but she watched as he turned and walked down the steps, starting off toward the diner and not looking back.

She snuggled down further in his sweatshirt and realized that she really wasn't cold any longer. Except maybe her toes. And so she sat down on the top step, absentmindedly scratching Billy's nose and looking up at the almost full moon. Maybe the darkness inside her didn't seem quite so heavy after talking with Zeke. In fact, she felt an almost happiness that she hadn't felt for a long time. She almost wished he'd come back.

Chapter 9

Bonnie Fox walked into the community center. She left her daughter, Annie, at home with the children and hadn't told her where she was going.

Normally, she tried to be considerate and make sure that Annie knew wherever she was. But this was rather important. Annie was obviously struggling, and the happiest that Bonnie had seen her was after she'd been with Zeke.

It had only been for a short while, but Bonnie was at the point she would grasp at any straw in order to try to help her daughter.

Since her daughter had refused counseling and would not consider medication, she was going to have to pull herself out of this funk on her own.

With a little nudge from her mother. And the Sweet Water matchmakers.

"Bonnie!" Miss April said, rising from her seat at the table where she was sewing squares together. "I'm so happy to see you. Is everything okay?"

Miss April added that last part, obviously concerned because Bonnie did not usually visit the community center.

She and Miss April saw each other at church, but with her accounting business, she'd never had time to come down to the community center and hang out even though she loved the ladies who were there.

"Everything's fine, but I do have a favor that I'd like to ask," she said as the other two ladies in the room, Miss June and Miss Helen, looked up from the crafting that they were doing to listen to the conversation.

Miss June looked rather haggard, with dark circles under her eyes, and she seemed like she'd aged a good bit since her cancer diagnosis three years ago.

Bonnie felt bad for her, because the rumor around town was that her husband had cheated or, at the very least, treated her terribly and was not kind to her. Bonnie couldn't imagine someone not loving Miss June, who always had a kind word for everyone. She'd never seen her upset, and even when she was sick, she had been sweet and patient.

Sometimes men just didn't seem to appreciate their wives. Maybe that was the problem with Miss June. Bonnie figured it probably wasn't her job to speculate.

Miss Helen, on the other hand, just glowed. She almost looked like a young girl in love and definitely a decade or more younger than her actual age. It was crazy what a good relationship could do to a person. That's why Bonnie had no trouble believing the reports that came out that said that people who were married lived longer. She suspected that if they checked on the actual relationship, there would be a correlation between a good relationship and a longer lifespan.

Not that it mattered to her, since she was not in a relationship and had no plans for one.

But she did have plans for Annie. If not to get in a relationship, at least to recover from the death of her husband. That had taken a hard toll on her, and as her mother, Bonnie figured it was her job to try to pull her daughter back from the edge of depression.

"We love helping people. Tell us what we can do," Miss April said, coming forward and giving her a hug which she returned, then drawing her further into the room.

Miss April sat down in front of the area where Miss June was working, and Miss Helen came over, carrying some flowers she was carefully snipping to just the right size.

"Well, you know my daughter has been struggling. We talked about that some at church. Now that she's moved here, I see that it's worse than what I thought. She doesn't even want to get out of bed in the morning."

"Has it been a year since her husband passed away?" Miss Helen asked, her voice heavy with concern.

"It has. I mean, everyone needs time to grieve, and people grieve in their own ways, but... I feel like it's time and it would be good for her to get out and about."

"I couldn't agree more," Miss April said. "What would you like us to do?"

"Well, the happiest I've seen her in the last year was the other day after she'd spoken with Zeke Butler. I... I wish there was some way we can get the two of them together." She sighed. "Even if it's not to match them up, just...to get Annie out again. Zeke was a friend of Merle, and I know Annie trusts him. And I know that he would be respectful toward her, even if he wasn't interested in a romance."

The ladies nodded, and some of the tightness in Bonnie's chest loosened. It was obvious that they were thinking, and if it was possible for them to help her, they would.

"I can try to get them together during the festival. I'm in charge of signing people up, and not all the slots are filled," Miss April said thoughtfully, tapping her chin with her first finger. "Do you ladies have any other ideas?"

"It would be nice if we could get them snowed in together," Miss Helen said with a smile.

"Considering that it's May, that might be a little bit difficult. Even if it is North Dakota. We might have to wait until at least October. But if we're still looking for ideas this fall, we could do that then."

"I have a friend who, if I remember correctly, Miss Bonnie, her son was related to Annie's husband. I can't remember exactly how, but they're in the Florida Keys on vacation. I know they have someone house-sitting... I don't know if we could work it to our advantage, but if we can somehow get Annie and Zeke there together, they wouldn't be snowed in, but they would be stuck together." She lifted her brows and sounded hopeful that the other ladies could take her idea and run with it.

"That would be awesome. If the people who are doing it somehow...couldn't do it anymore, and they were looking for someone to fill in..."

"But they wouldn't need two. Why would they need two people to watch their house?"

"It is a big house. And they do have animals. It's in Minnesota... It might be a wood-heated house. Annie might need help with the woodstove."

"Zeke could do that by himself."

"Maybe the lady wants to keep up on her cleaning?" Miss Helen said, sounding kind of lame.

But Bonnie snapped her fingers. "That could work. If there was just so much to do that they were looking for two people to do everything. Someone to take care of the outside animals and the woodstove, and someone to take care of the cooking... Is it far enough away from the store that they wouldn't be able to run to town to get food?"

"I can check, but I'm pretty sure it was very secluded, deep in the woods. So that actually might work." Miss Helen got her phone out and started swiping and clicking on it. "I'll just send them a text and see."

"Great. So, if that doesn't work, does anyone else have any other ideas?" Miss April asked hopefully.

"Zeke seems to be a little bit interested in her, but it might be just because he was Merle's friend, and you know how men can be.

They want to look after their friend's family, because they assume their friend would do that for them."

"Yeah, it's like a brotherhood code or something," Miss Helen said absently, pinching her nose.

"Hey! I think it might work. The people who are doing it are charging them, and my friend said that if we can get people to do it for free, that would be great."

"Is it far away from any stores?" Miss June asked, her brow wrinkling, like she'd latched onto that idea that there needed to be an excuse for Annie to go too.

Bonnie appreciated it, because she suspected that getting Zeke to go wouldn't be hard. He would be willing to help out wherever. But getting Annie to do it might be a little bit more difficult. She didn't seem to want to do anything lately.

"I think this will work," Miss Helen said as she read the text from her phone. "There are a lot of outside animals, several inside dogs, a couple of cats with a litter box, and the closest restaurant is an hour away. So unless they want to drive an hour each way, they need to get groceries and cook at the house. Oh, wait." She read a little more. "The house is actually stocked with groceries. But they have to cook there on their own, of course."

"That's perfect. So Annie could go to cook and clean, and Zeke could go to take care of the animals outside and to do the woodstove. Now..." Miss April looked at Bonnie. "We just need to figure out the best way to present this to them, and Annie in particular I'm guessing, to get them to say yes."

Chapter 10

"Hey there, what are you looking at?" Zeke said to the cow who stuck his nose next to the fence, took a deep breath, and blew it out.

When he had the wire pulled taunt and started pounding the staple in, the cow moved back.

He laughed. People didn't realize how curious cows were, but almost invariably if he was working out somewhere, they came over to check him out.

He had the staple pounded in when he felt his phone buzz in his pocket.

It was Saturday evening. He'd come out after supper to finish putting the fence up, since he'd be in town helping out with the festival all day Monday, and he didn't want to have to come home and chase cows.

Pulling his phone out of his pocket, he shoved his hammer in his tool belt and straightened up before swiping.

"Hello?"

"Zeke. This is Brett Delaney, we knew each other in the Air Force, although we were on different crews. I don't know if you remember me."

"Vaguely. You were related to Merle Brooks. A cousin or something." He just barely remembered Merle introducing them but couldn't really picture the man in his mind. "I'm sorry about your cousin."

"Yeah. It was a tragedy." The man was quiet for a minute, and then he totally changed the subject. "I have a small farm in the woods of Minnesota. Some cleared acreage, along with a lot of timber land. I have someone house-sitting for me, while my wife and I took a couple weeks of vacation in the Florida Keys. Unfortunately, the guy who I had flaked out on me, and I'm scrambling."

"Yeah. You have animals to feed?"

"I do. Right now, the neighbor's taking care of it, and he'll be able to do it through Monday, but then he's going back to his job in the Cities. One of those guys that go to their mountain getaway on the weekend. You know."

"Yeah. That's good." Zeke was happy the animals weren't going to starve. But he wasn't sure what the guy was getting at. He figured he'd eventually say something, so he shoved a hand in his pocket, leaned a hip against the fence post, and waited, watching the sun as it hovered just above the horizon, one last hurrah before it sank around the earth.

"Merle's wife, Annie, was good friends with my wife, and my wife talked to her mom, who said that she thought Annie would come out and help. She actually said she thought it would be good for Annie and her boys to take a little break and get away for a bit."

"Yeah. She probably needs a little change of scenery." She had just moved to North Dakota, but maybe having responsibilities like feeding animals and taking care of the house would snap her out of whatever lethargic mood she seemed to have fallen in.

"Her mom expressed concern that she wouldn't be able to handle everything. I have a few cows, some mules, and a couple of goats, and Annie is not a farm girl."

"Okay," Zeke said, unsure what else he was supposed to say when the man paused.

"Her mom suggested that you might be willing to drive her out and stay with her for a week until my wife and I get back. She said she didn't know you well enough to ask you herself and suggested that I probably should call and explain everything."

Zeke was quiet for a minute. The man was asking him to spend a week with Annie and her kids. Not like that would be a hardship or anything, but he wasn't sure how Annie was going to feel about that.

"I hated to ask someone to go by themselves, since it's rather remote and you have to cook your own meals, unless you want to drive an hour each way to the closest restaurant in town."

"I see."

"My wife had some light housekeeping she wanted done as well. Just making sure that the dogs make it outside and keeping any hair or anything swept up. We...really wanted a couple, but one that we knew. Not total strangers."

"Annie and I aren't a couple. You know it's only been a year since Merle passed."

"Well, plenty of people are remarried within a year, but I knew that. I understood you two to be friends though."

"Yeah. I guess." He wasn't sure whether he would label their relationship quite that familiarly or not. They sat on the porch swing together and talked without killing each other. If that made two people friends, then he supposed he and Annie qualified.

"Will you be able to get along for a week to house-sit in northern Minnesota? To be honest, I wouldn't want her to be there by herself. So if you don't think you can do it, it's fine. I just...will need to find someone else."

Zeke thought about that for all of a half a second.

He didn't suppose Annie would want to go to northern Minnesota to house-sit with a strange man, and he really didn't want her to. It wasn't hard for him to say the next words. "If Annie's in, I'm in too."

Chapter 11

"Last week when we walked to church, I lost you. I'll try to stay closer today, or do you think you can find Braden's room by yourself?" Annie's mom spoke to her as they stepped off the front porch on Sunday morning.

"I'm sorry. I wasn't expecting to stop and talk to anyone."

"I certainly wasn't expecting that either," her mom said, not without a little irony. "You know, if someone stops and asks you to help with something, why don't you just determine that you'll say yes. It'll be good for you."

"Mom. Did you forget? I might be house-sitting for Merle's cousin. I haven't heard back from him yet..." Her phone rang just as she was speaking. "That might be him now."

Her mom smiled. "Give me Braden's hand. I'll go on to church, and you can come along when you're done with your call."

Annie nodded, a little bit melancholy about how Braden so easily let go of her hand and grabbed her mother's.

She was glad they had a good relationship with her but felt like she was a little bit of a failure as a mom for her kids to not really care whether she came to church with them or not.

Maybe she did need to get up and be more involved.

She supposed that she just had to make herself do it, since no one else was going to. And if she waited until she had the motivation, she might never do it.

Swiping at her phone, she put it to her ear and said, "Hello?"

"Annie, it's Elaine. Your cousin's wife."

"Yes. I wondered if you might call me back. I was just talking to my mom about whether I should plan on being gone or not."

"Well, my husband spoke with Merle's friend Zeke last night, and he said he knew you, and if it was okay with you to go, he'd go too. I assume he would drive you both."

"Zeke?" Annie said, trying to keep the shocked surprise out of her voice. When she'd spoken with Elaine before, she had said she was going to talk to one of Merle's friends, but she didn't realize that friend was Zeke.

"You don't know him? Zeke Butler? He lives in Sweet Water according to my husband."

"I do. I do know him and..." She paused for just a minute. He couldn't have manipulated this. It wasn't possible. Not that she thought he did. It was just that he seemed to show up everywhere. And they'd come to a bit of a truce on the porch swing. In fact, she still had his sweatshirt in her room. She wasn't even going to try to get it back to him. She kind of liked it.

Which felt like a very junior high thing to do, but...maybe there was a part of her that had never outgrown junior high.

"And I'm fine with that," she said. She didn't want to go house-sit in the woods by herself. Actually, she didn't want to go at all. But she could hardly turn Merle's cousin down. She and Elaine had been good friends since they got married, and... She found herself, if not wanting to go, at least not completely hating the idea. In fact, she couldn't quite label the feeling she had excitement, but there was definitely a part of her that was looking forward to spending an entire week with Zeke.

At the very least, he'd make her laugh. And she felt safe with him.

"All right. Like I said, my husband already talked to Zeke. And I wanted to make sure that you and I were on the same page. I can have him call Zeke and see if Zeke will get a hold of you somehow."

"I should see him at church today. I can talk to him then."

"All right. That's perfect. We'll make sure to text you directions and expect you guys to show up Monday night?"

"We'll see. We have a festival on Monday, and I know Zeke has committed to helping with it. We can leave after that, depending on how long it will take to get there."

"All right. That sounds good. I'll tell my husband and stay in touch if anything comes up, okay?"

"All right."

Annie swiped her phone off and took a minute to pet Billy who stood on the sidewalk in what had become his normal spot.

"Zeke is right. Why are you always standing at my house?" Annie murmured, scratching between his ears and careful to dodge his horns as he moved his head back and forth.

His eyes looked placid and serene. Certainly not the eyes of a calculating matchmaker who watched people and tried to fix them up with each other.

The idea was ludicrous. A sane person could not look at this unintelligent bovine, whose only concern was getting food in his stomach, and think that he had anything to do with people falling in love and getting married.

It was crazy to think what small towns made up in order to put themselves on the map.

Annie shook her head, told Billy to go find someone else to match because he was wasting his time with her, and then turned and walked toward the church.

She wasn't sure which vehicle was Zeke's, so she didn't spend time looking in the parking lot to see if she could tell whether he was there or not.

But her eyes scanned the people who were walking in.

His blond hair wasn't hard to pick out, and she walked quickly, passing several people and waving at them as she hurried to catch up with him.

He was laughing with another man and a couple when she tapped him on the shoulder.

"Excuse me?"

He turned around so quickly she took a step back.

"Annie? Is everything okay?"

"Yeah. Can I talk to you for a minute?"

"Sure."

He turned back to the people he was talking with. "I'll be in in a bit."

He didn't wait for their response before he turned back to her.

"Do you want to walk this way?" He pointed toward the large oak tree that had been planted years ago and the small cemetery that grew by a dozen or so tombstones every year.

"Yeah. This would be fine."

There was a bench under the oak tree, but he walked past it, and she appreciated that. She didn't want to sit down. She squeezed her hands in front of her as he headed toward the last row of gravestones.

"Are your kids okay?"

"Mom has them. She took them to Sunday school."

"Oh. Good."

Annie groaned, wondering why she all of a sudden felt...shy. She pushed that feeling aside. There was nothing to be afraid of. "I got a call from Elaine. Merle's cousin's wife. I think you knew Merle's cousin from the Air Force?"

"I do. And I got a call from him last night."

"They said you agreed to house-sit as long as I went, too?"

"I hope that didn't sound too bad. I just meant that I didn't want them to find someone that you didn't know, and you'd be stuck for a week in a house with a stranger."

Of course. That was the kind of consideration she was starting to expect from Zeke. She was a little disappointed. Maybe she wanted him to admit that he liked her and wanted to spend time with her.

Was that so terrible? She could hardly believe she was thinking along those lines. But she found it to be true.

"Thank you. I appreciate you being considerate like that. Because you're right. I don't want to end up sharing a house with a man I don't know. Although, I should hope that Elaine and her husband wouldn't leave me stuck with someone who was dangerous."

"Just someone you would eat for breakfast with your standoffish attitude. Someone who wouldn't be persistent enough to get around it."

"Oh. So you aren't actually doing it for me, you're doing it to save someone from me?" She was teasing, mostly. Although it was a little bit hurtful.

"No. I said yes because I wanted to. The idea of being with you for a week is not unpleasant."

"All right. That's a little better."

"I wasn't doing it because of Merle. It's not anything to do with him. Just to be clear."

"I did accuse you of that, didn't I?"

"You did. And you were right at first. Obviously he was my friend, I wanted to make sure you're okay, but it's not that anymore."

Her heart skipped a beat. And she hid a smile. That's what she wanted to hear. That he was with her because he wanted to be and not out of a sense of duty.

"I'm not sure what he talked to you about, but Elaine wanted us there tomorrow night if possible."

"We can leave after the festival. I think the drive is six or eight hours."

"That's what I thought. But since you'll probably be driving... Unless you want to drive separately?" She hoped not. She had driven from Indiana to North Dakota, but she hadn't enjoyed it.

"I assumed we'd go together. That just makes sense. And I didn't know if you'd bring the kids along or not, but I figured they would enjoy it. It sounded like there'd be lots of animals and woods to explore. There's probably a creek to play in as well."

"Oh. I think they would love that. I hadn't even considered taking them. But that would give Mom a break from us."

"I think she loves having you there. She definitely looks happy with your kids chattering on either side of her. She's a proud grandma."

"That's a relief. I feel like we're imposing at times. Like we're interrupting her empty-nest years."

"I don't think so. But you're probably right that she would enjoy a break."

"All right. If you don't mind having such a long ride with little kids. They can make it challenging."

"Pretty sure I can handle it. I managed to live in barracks with hundreds of other men and learned to tune pretty much anything out. I'm sure the kids are not gonna bother me."

She had her doubts. Kids could irritate even the most patient of people. But she appreciated him being willing to try, even if he really didn't have any idea what he was getting himself into.

But then she remembered that some of the men who lived out on Sweet Briar Ranch had children, so Zeke maybe did have an idea of what he was getting into.

"All right. Then we'll figure out what time you're getting done tomorrow, and we'll leave...as soon as you're ready?"

"That sounds good. I'm sure we'll see each other around tomorrow, but if not, I have your phone number."

"Indeed you do."

She smiled when she thought of how he got it. And she wanted to apologize again for being unkind. To explain that she normally wasn't that way, but she just felt such hopeless darkness and maybe even a lot of resentment.

She looked out over the gravestones, thinking about life and how the people whose names were on those tombstones had a chance to live once, but now their chance was over.

Did she really want to spend most of her life being depressed and sad? Did she want to waste it that way?

If the people in the ground could talk to her, she'd be willing to bet that they would say that life is too short, too precious, to allow feelings of gloom and doom to overtake a person. That it was more fun to look on the bright side and to force herself if necessary to get up and get moving. This trip seemed like just the thing.

Of course, maybe, as her mom suggested, she should try counseling again. Perhaps medication would work.

Or maybe, she wasn't that far gone. Maybe, this was just what she needed to get her life back on track and to pull herself out of the hole where she'd fallen.

"Are you ready to walk back?" Zeke finally said, as he too seemed to look over the graveyard, in some kind of contemplation, although he didn't say what.

"I am." She took a breath. "Thanks for not giving up on me."

"Hey, I'd like it if someone would do the same for me. Give me a little grace when I'm maybe not at my best."

She nodded, smiling a bit. Liking that that was the way he looked at it. Not that she was a nasty person that he had to love anyway, but that even good people had bad days. Or a lot of bad days.

She supposed maybe she should change her outlook. And make it so that instead of seeing people and thinking of them as grumpy or mean, she'd start thinking of them as nice people who were just having a hard time.

They turned around and started walking back toward the church together.

As they walked, their knuckles brushed, and it shocked Annie that she was tempted to twist her hand and allow their fingers to tangle together.

Instead, she reached up to her shoulder and adjusted her purse strap.

She hadn't considered holding hands with any man since her husband had died. Was she really thinking about that with Zeke?

The thought startled her. Not only did it feel like the dark fog around her brain was lifting, but it felt like the ice around her heart might be melting as well. Maybe the two were connected.

Chapter 12

Annie held Justin's hand in one hand and Braden's hand in the other as they walked to the Sweet Water Memorial Day festival.

Her mom had been roped into helping in the kitchen, and so Annie was on her own.

She felt tired and definitely did not feel like walking around the festival with her children.

But from the smiles on their faces, they were loving it, and she couldn't resist doing something so simple that made them happy.

"Annie!" Miss April said, hurrying up beside her. "Have you signed up for the wheelbarrow race? Are you going to participate? I mean, I think your children would love it."

"Sure. I'm feeling a little overwhelmed. There's so much stuff." There were people milling around everywhere, and different booths and activities going on all around.

"Nobody gave you a schedule?" Miss April whipped one out of her purse and handed it over. "The wheelbarrow race is just getting started, and I know that you guys are just going to love it."

Miss April held her hand out, and Justin gripped it, grinning up into the lady's face.

"You want to win the wheelbarrow race, don't you?" Miss April said to the little boy. "If you win, you get a watermelon!"

Annie bit back a laugh. A watermelon? That seemed like an odd prize, but it made Justin's eyes go big, and he eagerly followed Miss

April as she led him across the trampled grass that, on normal days, was a hayfield just outside of town.

"I want watermelon!" Braden said, looking up at his mom and tugging gently on her hand.

"You know, I wouldn't mind having one either," Annie said, thinking that whoever came up with the prize really should get an award for that. Who wouldn't want to win a watermelon?

It was certainly a better prize than a trophy that would end up sitting in someone's garage for the next two decades before someone threw it away.

"Let's go!" Braden said with excitement.

They turned and followed Miss April, hurrying to catch up to her.

It wasn't hard to see the wheelbarrow race.

There were actual wheelbarrows. For some reason, she was thinking it was going to be the kind of race where she held someone's feet while they walked with their hands.

But apparently, a person got in the wheelbarrow, and someone was going to be pushing.

She could only imagine who that was going to be.

As the mom, she was sure she was going to be the pusher.

But as they got to the starting line, Miss April was assigning each of her boys a wheelbarrow in the line of ten.

"Now, Justin, you sit here in this wheelbarrow, and Mr. Martin is going to push you. Can you say hi to Mr. Martin?" Miss April said.

Justin dutifully said, "Hi, Mr. Martin."

It looked like she wasn't going to have to push the boys after all, Annie thought to herself as Miss April did the same thing with Braden, leading him to his wheelbarrow, introducing him to his pusher, and then coming back to Annie.

"Whoever decided to offer a watermelon as a prize was a pretty smart person," Annie said as Miss April came back.

"Mom! You said you wanted to win a watermelon too!" Braden yelled at Annie.

"Did she now?" Miss April said, turning to Braden. Her brows lifted as she met his eyes. "That's fortunate, because I actually have you on the schedule as well." She took a hold of Annie's elbow and led her three wheelbarrows down.

"You've already met Zeke," Miss April said.

Annie, bemused, had been trying to figure out how to get out of it but had allowed Miss April to grab her elbow and lead her to wheelbarrow. She balked when Miss April stopped and mentioned Zeke.

"I was just kidding about the watermelon," Annie said, lifting her hand and giving Zeke a little wave, but focusing all of her attention on Miss April. She didn't want to get suckered into awkwardly sitting in a wheelbarrow and getting pushed around what looked like an obstacle course.

"That's fine. I guess if my push-ee is not cooperating, I can sit this race out," Zeke said. Sweat beaded on his brow, showing this was not the first race he'd run.

"Have you been doing this all morning?"

"This is my fifth race. And last," he said, looking at Miss April who nodded her head.

"He's scheduled to go to the dunking booth next. So, this is his last chance to win."

"I hardly think he's gonna win with me in the wheelbarrow. After all, he's racing against people who are pushing a three-year-old and a four-year-old."

Miss April sighed, shook her head, and looked at Zeke. "I think she's questioning your manhood."

Annie had to work not to roll her eyes. She wasn't questioning anyone's manhood. She was just pointing out that there was a weight difference between herself and her three-year-old.

"I noticed that. It was very hurtful," Zeke said, as though she had deliberately insulted him.

"I'm sorry. I didn't mean to hurt you. I was just—"

"If you're truly sorry, you need to get in the wheelbarrow and take up your spot. Give Zeke his last chance to win."

"You know, I was really looking forward to that watermelon." Zeke's look of disappointment almost seemed real.

"If you haven't won the last four times, I'm pretty sure you're not going to win with me," Annie said, realizing that she probably had already lost the argument but unable to get her mouth to stop.

"I am sad that you don't have any confidence in me," Zeke said, pressing his lips together and shaking his head.

"Okay let's do this," Miss April said, her hands on her hips, looking between Zeke and Annie. "Zeke hasn't won a race today yet. And you don't feel like he is capable of winning this one either. I say, that if Zeke manages to win this race with you in the wheelbarrow, you will give him a kiss as his prize along with his watermelon."

Miss April brushed her hands down her pants and gave a short nod. "There. Now that's settled. Get in the wheelbarrow, because it's about to start."

Annie had her mouth open to protest. Not necessarily because she found Zeke offensive, exactly, she just didn't go around kissing random men. But she closed it. She wasn't going to say anything else, since it seemed like everything that came out of her mouth was an insult. And since she had already declared her opinion that Zeke wasn't going to win, protesting the kiss was most likely a moot point, since the odds of him winning were very small.

"Line up at the starting line with your wheelbarrows, front tire on the white line." George Finkenbinder's voice sounded tinny as he spoke through the megaphone.

"You look pretty distressed over the kissing. Let's do it like this. If I lose, you'll owe me a kiss. That way, I'll try hard to win just to keep you from having to do something you don't want to do. Deal?" Zeke said as he put his hands on the wheelbarrow handles to steady it while Annie climbed in.

"But I don't think you're going to win!" she said, then she clapped a hand over her mouth. She wasn't going to say anything.

"All right. We'll just leave it the way it is. And I'll go slow."

She shook her head and looked back at him. He didn't seem like the kind of man who wasn't going to try as hard as he could in order to win.

She hadn't watched any of the other races, although now she wished she would have. Then she'd have a little better idea of which way she wanted to go.

"So you think I'm less likely to have to kiss you if you lose, or are you saying that I'll do it if you lose?" She couldn't believe she was having this conversation. Normal people didn't do this type of thing, right? Except Miss April acted like she did this type of thing all the time.

Maybe that's what matchmakers in a small town did, but Annie wasn't really that kind of person.

"I think maybe we might be pulling on opposite sides for this anyway," Zeke said rather enigmatically as the man with the megaphone spoke again.

"Participants, take your mark, get set, go!" A small gunshot sounded as he said the word "go," and Zeke picked the wheelbarrow up and started running with it.

Annie squealed, and her hands came out, clasping either side. She hadn't exactly been ready. She certainly hadn't gotten herself situated and felt like she was going to fall out at any minute.

She squeezed her eyes shut tightly as Zeke swerved hard to miss a fellow contestant and also make it around the hay bale that had been set up in the middle of the course.

Annie squeezed one eye open in time to see that they barely cleared the hay bale, and there were three more scattered ahead of them, as well as an old wagon, a barrel of some type, and two flagpoles.

"You can slow down," she said, wishing she had kept her mouth closed, because she didn't exactly want to lose, but she also felt like she was going to go flying out of the wheelbarrow.

"Hold on. Jump," Zeke said tersely before the wheelbarrow went flying up in the air.

Annie knew they couldn't possibly be going that fast, but it felt like she was flying at freeway speeds as the wheelbarrow bounced back down.

She managed to not bang her head against the back of it, but she never did quite figure out how.

"Leaning left!" Zeke shouted, and before Annie could figure out which side was her right and which side was her left and whether they were actually turning right or turning left, the wheelbarrow leaned, almost spilling her out.

She held tight and swallowed the scream that clung to her throat, clawing for air.

She couldn't tell whether they were in front or not. She actually couldn't see anyone else around them at all. With her eyes closed, she couldn't see much of anything.

She cracked one lid just in time to see a wheelbarrow looming up in front of them.

She couldn't quite swallow that scream as the wheelbarrow lurched to the side, leaning first one way then the other.

"Hang tight, we're doing a U-y," Zeke said as the wheelbarrow completely shifted directions.

Now she understood why they offered watermelon as a prize. No one would do this if the prize wasn't something really, really good.

She wasn't even sure a watermelon was worth it. It better be a big one.

The wheelbarrow swerved first right and left, with Zeke calling out a warning each time, but Annie was unable to figure out which side was right and which was left because it seemed like when they went to the right, she had to hold onto the left, and she had never been very good with those directions anyway.

"Going under the waterfall," Zeke said, which made Annie's eyes pop open.

"What?" she barked out, just before they went between two rows of stacked hay bales, where a couple of teenage boys were sitting at the top with buckets of water that they dumped on people as they went through the tunnel formed by the bales.

"Aaaah!" she cried, not realizing that it wasn't a normal, run-of-the-mill wheelbarrow race. But obstacle course and water ride all in one.

Water sloshed around the bottom of the wheelbarrow as they lurched to the side.

"Rats! I about fall there every time," Zeke exclaimed as he seemed to catch his balance, and the wheelbarrow only slowed for just a second. "Hang on. Straight shot to the end."

Annie cracked her eyes again and noticed that there was a wheelbarrow, with Braden in it, of all people, running right beside them.

She kind of wanted Braden to win the watermelon, but if he did, he might not share with Justin, so it might be better if she won.

She hadn't quite gotten that idea settled in her brain when they broke through the ribbon that was stretched across the finish line, and her wheelbarrow stopped, right in front of a smiling Miss April.

"I knew you could do it, Zeke!" Miss April said.

As Annie pried her eyes open, she realized Miss April was holding a watermelon.

"All right, you two get to share this, since we only have one."

After all that, risking her life, getting soaking wet, and surviving with no major head injuries, she had to share her watermelon?

Chapter 13

Zeke took the watermelon from Miss April. "Thank you," he said.

He'd seen other people being awarded their watermelons at the finish line, and he laughed a little. A watermelon was such a crazy, perfect prize.

But for each of the first four races, he'd had a little girl in his wheelbarrow, and he hadn't wanted to hurt anyone or have them fall out or even scare them too much. He didn't want them to cry. He wouldn't know what to do with a crying child.

With Annie, he felt like he could take a few more risks and go a little faster. Although he had almost wiped out after they went through the water tunnel, where the ground was slick and they had to make a 90° turn, but he'd managed to catch himself on one knee, get back up, and keep running.

"You won it," Annie said, looking up at him in an accusatory way. Like that was the whole point.

"So did you. And this is yours," he said, thinking maybe she was upset because he looked like he was going to take the whole watermelon for himself. It was way too big for one person to eat all in one sitting.

"But you hadn't won any of the previous four races."

Before he could explain why that was, Braden came running over.

"Mom! Mom! You won! Are you sharing your watermelon?"

He hopped into the wheelbarrow, trying to climb onto his mom's lap.

"Hey, bud. Let me out of here."

"I want a piece of watermelon!"

"Mom. How did you guys win?" Justin said, coming over and looking at the watermelon, and sharing the excitement of his little brother.

"I guess he was the fastest."

"I've done the course four times. I think I knew it better than anyone else, and I trusted your mom not to let go and fall out."

"I would've gotten run over if I had fallen out," she said, sounding a little bit irritated as Braden got out of the wheelbarrow, and she threw a leg over, looking back at him to see if he was going to balance the wheelbarrow and make sure it didn't fall over while she got out.

He carefully held the watermelon in one hand, although it was slippery since he was wet, and put a hand on the handle of the wheelbarrow.

"You can get out now," he said easily.

"You gonna share with us, Mom? We haven't had watermelon in a long time," Justin said, looking longingly at the green fruit.

"If it's okay with your mom, find a picnic table and sit down, and I'll share."

"That's fine with me," Annie said. "As long as you don't mind?"

"I don't mind at all. It's yours too."

"It does look good," Annie said, still not looking like she felt like the ride had been worth it.

He had been careful, but...maybe it was what Miss April said about the kiss. Or maybe it was just the idea that he wanted to win because of Annie.

She wasn't going to say anything about the kiss, and he wasn't either. That was just Miss April being Miss April.

"Can we sit at that table right there?" Justin said, pointing to an empty picnic table just a little bit away.

"Sure, if that's okay with you?" Annie asked, looking at him.

"Good with me. If it's still empty when we get there."

Both of the boys took off toward the table, while he and Annie followed at a more leisurely pace.

"I guess I owe you a kiss," Annie muttered.

"Ah, a woman who pays her debts. I like it."

"What's that supposed to mean?" she asked with a little bit of a laugh. Maybe it was a nervous laugh.

"I wasn't going to remind you of that. I thought it didn't seem like something you really wanted to do to begin with, and I honestly wasn't expecting to win. It's true that I've done it four times and lost all four times, but each time, they put a cute little girl in my wheelbarrow, and I couldn't go as fast as I wanted to because I figured she'd be scared. And I didn't want her to get hurt."

"All right. I'm trying not to be offended over that. Because obviously, you don't think I'm cute, or little, and apparently...not a girl."

"You're a woman. I wasn't questioning your gender," Zeke said firmly.

She laughed. "I was mostly teasing you. I understand now why you didn't win before."

"Yeah. I didn't have enough time at the starting line to explain that to you. And that was kind of why I tried to change the bet. Because I thought maybe I had a shot."

"I see," Annie said, and then she added, "Still, a deal is a deal. I want to be the kind of person who keeps my word and pays my debts, as you said."

They got to the table then, and he didn't say anything else. He didn't want to embarrass her. And he wasn't going to require that payment. She could forfeit or substitute with something else, but that wasn't a conversation they would have in front of her children.

"I can eat half of it myself," Justin said.

"Well, even if you could, you wouldn't, because you want to make sure you share with everyone. So at the very most, you would eat one fourth so that everyone gets the same amount," Annie explained to her son.

She looked better than he had ever seen her. Her eyes were bright, her hair a little windblown, and her cheeks red. A lot better than the lethargic, almost sick-looking woman he sat on the swing with.

He kinda thought the wheelbarrow race had been good for her, and he wondered if Miss April had done it on purpose.

The boys climbed up to the big table and sat down on their knees, their hands on the table, their eyes glued to the watermelon.

"Do we have something to cut it with?" Annie asked, biting her lip.

"I have a pocketknife, but it probably wouldn't hurt for it to be wiped off."

"I always carry wipes with me," Annie said, pulling a little pouch of wipes out of the small bag she'd been carrying.

He supposed with children wipes were something that a person just naturally had.

Their fingers brushed as he took it from her, and a strange sensation flew up his arm.

He enjoyed her company, and felt a strange tug toward her, and now... There was some kind of odd feeling when he touched her.

He shook it off, figuring that maybe it had something to do with the excitement of winning the race.

After he cleaned his knife, he cut into the watermelon and handed everyone a nice thick slice.

"It's a juicy one anyway," he said as the boys started eating.

"It looks good," Annie said as he handed her her slice.

It might have been his imagination, but she seemed to take care to take the slice from him on the opposite side from which he was holding it.

That made him wonder if she felt the same thing he had and hadn't wanted to repeat the experience.

He pushed that thought aside, sliced up one for himself, and bit into it.

Sweet, sticky juice slid down his chin as he smiled at the taste.

It was a good one.

"Was it worth the crazy ride?" he asked Annie.

"Well, considering that Braden came in second, I would be eating watermelon regardless of whether or not we won."

He laughed. She was right, and he hadn't even thought about that.

"Actually, you wouldn't have been, because I had the knife."

"We could have borrowed it."

"And I would have required payment of at least a slice of watermelon in order to allow you to use it. So, regardless of your ride, I would have been eating watermelon too."

"All right. I'll give you that, but the ride didn't need to have been so wild."

"Why not, Mommy? It was fun!" Justin said before he chomped another bite of his watermelon.

"Maybe for you. But I didn't like getting wet."

"Oh boy. Speaking of getting wet, I'm due at the dunking booth in just a few minutes. If you don't mind, I'm going to need to run." He looked at the watermelon and his knife sitting on the table. "I can leave my knife here, if you give it back to me when you're done with it."

"We can do that. Cut yourself off another piece," Annie offered as he finished up the one in his hand.

"Actually, I don't mind if I do. It's a good watermelon."

"Best one I've had in a long time. Of course, I haven't eaten one since last summer."

"Same. I guess maybe the first one of the year always tastes the best."

"Maybe," Annie said, and he liked that she didn't just blindly agree with him. She was probably right. Sometimes the first watermelons of the year could be rather tasteless and not sweet at all.

He finished slicing his piece, lay his knife beside the watermelon, and stood. "Thanks for holding on, it would have been terrible if I'd spilled you. If you want to bring the boys down to the dunking booth, I think for a quarter they could throw a ball at the handle and see if they can dump me."

"Oh! I want to do that, Mom!" Braden exclaimed.

"I want to be in the dunking booth. Can I?" Justin said, causing Zeke to laugh.

"If I could trade places with you, trust me. I would."

"No. You can't be in the dunking booth. Maybe when you get older. You could put your request in to Miss April next time you see her, and I'm sure she'll keep you in mind when you get a little bit bigger."

"I'm big now," Justin said, tapping on his chest.

"You're big enough to throw balls and to try to dunk Mr. Zeke," Annie said calmly.

"Can I have some more watermelon, please?" Braden asked, inching toward it while he asked.

"You sure can," she said, picking up the knife. "I'll make sure you get this back. And it sounds like we'll definitely be down to the dunking booth. Where is it?"

He pointed it out and then waved goodbye, walking down through the crowd.

He always had a good time when he was with her. He liked how calm she was with her children and how she pushed any issues that she was having aside in order to do the best for them. The fact that she was even here for the festival showed that she cared about her kids and put them first.

He found himself wanting to whistle as he walked down through the hayfield, nodding at the townspeople he knew and even the folks he didn't. Every year, the festival got bigger, and Sweet Water was almost overrun with people

He made a detour around the tractor driving contest, where Palmer, who lived just outside of town, was driving and his wife was picking up hay bales.

They looked like they were having fun, and people from the crowd were hollering encouragement, sounding mostly like they were encouraging Palmer to go faster to make Ames work harder.

There was a lot of bantering back and forth, and Zeke felt a small squeeze in his chest. That was the kind of marriage he wanted. Where, as they approached middle age, they were still laughing and having fun with each other. Doing things together and looking for all the world like they were teenagers still in love and still having fun together.

He supposed he hadn't thought a whole lot about the kind of marriage that he wanted throughout his life. Or even about getting married. Life had always been about working hard and doing his best and eventually owning a ranch, combined with his love of flying.

But maybe being around Annie, or maybe it was her children, had gotten him thinking in a different way.

Once he reached the small tent behind the dunking booth, he grabbed the shorts and T-shirt he'd set aside earlier and changed into them.

He reached the booth just in time as the person before him, a teenager who had graduated from high school just a week ago, was climbing down.

"My time is up, I was leaving whether you came or not," the kid said as he met Zeke who was standing at the back of the tank.

"I'm here, and it's a good thing. Looks like you got a line."

"I do, but thankfully nobody has very good aim," he said. And that's when Zeke noticed that the kid was still dry.

It gave him hope. He hadn't been looking forward to being dumped in the cold water. It was only May, and the air temperature might have been seventy-five. Not really warm enough to go for a swim. In his estimation anyway.

The scent of cotton candy and hot dogs wafted through the air as he climbed up onto the seat and settled down carefully, not wanting to take a swim before he needed to.

Thankfully the latch was sturdy, which might have been part of the problem since people would have to hit the lever rather hard in order to get it to disengage.

Maybe he could fix that. But not until after his turn was over. He'd see how it went.

The line went through fairly quickly, and he had a good time laughing and joking with people as they attempted to throw the ball hard enough and with accuracy in order to hit the circle which would disengage the lever.

"Looks like you're having fun?" a familiar voice said, and he looked at the next kid in line. Braden.

He smiled as Annie nodded at her son and then looked up at him.

"I'm still dry," he said. "Actually, I'm more dry with this than I was with the wheelbarrow race."

"I see that. Maybe we can fix that for you," she said, and he huffed out a laugh.

He was pretty sure that Braden was not going to hit anything, unless it was a major accident. Probably the same for Justin, since he was just a little bit older.

Annie handed balls to each of the boys, and they threw them, not even coming close.

"Boys, I think you need to give your mom a turn," he joked when both of them had thrown their three allotted balls.

"I hardly think I'll do any better than they do."

"You try, Mommy. Mr. Zeke needs to get wet."

"You've raised some heartless children," he said in reply to Braden's observation.

"I raised children who obviously have an eye for needs in the neighborhood," Annie joked right back to him.

But she didn't argue further and paid for three balls for herself.

She held a ball in her right hand, closing one eye as though eyeing up the bull's-eye. "It's been a long time since I've thrown a ball. I think I will consider the first one a practice ball."

She squinted at the target, drew her hand back, and threw while stepping forward. She must have tripped on something, he wasn't sure, but the ball lobbed up in the air and would have hit him on the head if he hadn't snatched it out of the air.

"Yeah. I don't think I have to worry about getting wet with this one," he said, catching the attendant's eye and lobbing the ball back over the Plexiglas walls of the tank.

"That was just my practice throw. I'm getting warmed up."

"All right. I'm kinda curious to see where the next one goes. I think there's a hot dog vendor down the way that might catch one for you."

"Very funny," Annie said, and then she got a serious, concentrating look on her face as she eyed the target and pulled her hand back again.

"Throw hard, Mommy!" Braden said as she stepped forward to throw.

Maybe he distracted her, or maybe she really couldn't throw balls.

Zeke figured that not everyone had a dad like he did, who stood out in the yard and tossed the ball back and forth after school and work.

Whatever it was, that ball went backward.

"Remind me never to take you bowling," Zeke murmured.

"That would have been worse with a bowling ball, wouldn't it?" Annie said, appearing unfazed by the fact that neither one of her balls had gone anywhere near where they were supposed to.

In fact, she almost looked like she was having a good time.

He liked the glow in her eyes and her red cheeks.

"Folks, maybe you'd better stand back," Zeke said as Annie rolled the last ball in her hand.

"Mommy. You're supposed to try to get that red spot right there," Justin said in an apparent effort to be helpful.

"The red spot?" Annie asked with a brow raised, like she hadn't known. "All right. I'll hit the red spot this time."

"Interesting, I can't imagine what you had been aiming at, considering you threw one ball forward and one ball backward."

"It's a moving target," Annie said casually.

"It's stationary," Zeke replied.

"Please be quiet. I'm trying to concentrate," Annie said, her brow raised disdainfully.

Zeke closed his mouth, but he couldn't keep from lifting the corners of his lips up.

She was too cute.

This time when she threw the ball, she didn't trip, and her son's voice didn't interrupt her. However, the ball went slightly left and sailed past the dunking tank, whizzing over and bumping against a tree, zinging back, and hitting the Plexiglas wall before dropping to the ground.

Zeke couldn't help it; he laughed. "I kinda thought I was safe on that one."

"All right. I'm calling rank here. Taunting by the dunk-ee. The ball thrower can come in and manually move the knob." The pimple-faced attendant gave Zeke a superior grin.

"Really?" Annie said as the attendant opened the gate and motioned for her to go in.

Her boys, jumping up and down by her side, walked in after her.

"Just hold on here a second, that wasn't in the contract," Zeke said, knowing there had been no contract but that the attendant was just making things up. "That wasn't fair."

"I'm in charge. Miss April said that whatever I say goes. So, I say she gets a free dunk because of taunting." The kid lifted his shoulder and motioned for Annie to go ahead.

Annie shook her head. "Oh, I couldn't—"

But her kids could. They both had their hands on the knob and pushed as hard as they could. That was the last thing Zeke saw before he splashed into the tank.

He came up sputtering. He should have been paying attention to the kids and not to Annie, and then it wouldn't have been such a shock that he slid into the water.

The two-by-four wasn't sanded very well either; he thought he had a splinter in his rear.

But Annie was laughing, and he kinda felt like the whole thing was worth it.

"You'd better save me some watermelon. You owe me after that."

"You're right. I do. I'm sorry, I really wasn't going to dunk you, but..."

And that made him wonder if maybe she'd thrown the balls all those wacked-out ways on purpose.

He laughed. He kinda liked having a woman he couldn't figure out.

Chapter 14

Annie sat at the picnic table, waiting for Zeke to show up. He'd texted her twenty minutes before and said that his time in the dunking booth was up, and he'd be changing his clothes and heading back up to the picnic table if she wanted to share the rest of her watermelon.

She had wrapped it and put it in the refrigerator at the community center so the flies wouldn't get it while they were at the dunking booth, and the kids participated in several other fun contests, and Justin had sat still to get his face painted.

Braden hadn't accomplished that feat, but he had a small football painted on his hand.

Regardless, she needed to apologize. She hadn't meant to dunk Zeke at all. She'd actually purposely thrown the ball in really weird directions so that she didn't accidentally hit the button to dump him.

She figured someone else could do it, but it wasn't going to be her.

She had thought it wasn't going to be her children either. Well, that was a surprise anyway.

Zeke strolled over, and he was grinning. She had to return the smile.

She hadn't realized until just then, but she felt better that day than she'd felt in a long time. And for the first time in a while, she realized she was admiring a man. The way he walked, just competent and relaxed, like he was ready to handle whatever got thrown at him. Of course, it helped that he looked good in his jeans and T-shirt, and the boots added a great touch.

She drew her eyes away, looking back down at the watermelon and cutting off a piece for him. There wasn't much left, and she was kind of happy she wasn't going to have to drag it all home. It had been fun to snack on it throughout the day.

"So not only did you get me completely soaking wet, but you ate all of my watermelon too," Zeke said as he strolled over and took the watermelon from her.

As she had done, he took it from the opposite side from where she held it.

It had felt odd when their fingers touched, and she hadn't wanted to examine that too carefully, so she'd been trying to avoid having it happen again.

Maybe he was doing the same.

The idea intrigued her but not enough for her to say anything about it. That would be an awkward conversation.

As awkward as the one about her owing him a kiss. It was all in fun, but even in fun, she'd never not paid a debt.

"You're eating watermelon, aren't you?" she asked as he took a bite.

"The watermelon I won," he said with his mouth full.

"Don't talk with your mouth full. It makes Mom mad," Justin said, speaking with his mouth full.

"Justin," Annie said with a warning note in her voice.

His eyes got big, and his mouth clamped shut. He swallowed, stretching his neck out, as though to make sure he got everything that was in his mouth down before he said, "Sorry."

She always wanted to laugh when her kids did things like that. They were just so cute. But she tried to keep her mom look on her face so he wouldn't think that she was just joking about not talking with his mouth full.

It was a bad habit, and as cute as he was at this age, it wasn't going to be cute when he was older.

They chatted for a little bit before the kids got up and asked if they could go play at the playground they could see from where they were sitting.

"Sure, just be sure that you're kind to the other kids," Annie reminded them before they took off.

Zeke had gotten up to throw all the watermelon rinds in the closest garbage can. He came back and sat down.

"We planning on leaving in a bit?" he asked as he watched the children run to the playground.

"I think so. It's good for me if we do. They've not had naps, and they've been on the go all day. I think it won't be long till they fall asleep, and that should make it an easier ride."

He nodded. "I don't know much about that, so I'll take your word for it."

"All right. I'm all packed. So I think all we'll need to do is maybe give the kids baths? If we have time. That way, we won't have to worry about cleaning them up when we get there."

"All right. So..." He checked his watch. "I don't know how long all that will take, so can you give me an idea? And if there's anything I can do to help you, I'd be happy to."

"No. I think I'll be good. I'll just let them play for a little bit if you don't mind, and then take them home, clean them up, and that should be about an hour. But I'll text you."

"I've got all of my stuff with me, and I don't need to go back home, so unless you have a problem with it, I'll just hang out with you. If you'd rather do it by yourself, I can go find something to do for an hour."

She smiled, maybe at the thought that he didn't mind spending time with her, or maybe at the idea that he could help.

Her mom had been awesome, but it was nice to have a friend giving her a hand.

If that's what Zeke was, a friend.

"That's fine with me. I just don't want you to miss out on anything, if you'd rather be doing something else."

He was a single man, who probably had plenty of things he'd rather do than hang out with a woman and her two small children. She felt compelled to add, "I promise no one will be upset if you don't come sit with me for the next hour."

"I thought we were already through this. I'm here because I enjoy your company."

He didn't have any irritation in his voice, and he seemed to be willing to say that to her as many times as she needed to hear it.

"I'm sorry. I just find it really hard to believe. I'm not exactly an entertaining person, and in fact, I'm a little bit depressing to be around. And hanging out with small children isn't exactly every man's dream."

"No. I have to agree with that. I definitely haven't dreamed about hanging out with small kids, but I'm kind of enjoying you and your kids. Is that so terrible?"

"Oh, stop. I'm going to get a big head."

He laughed. Maybe, if he kept telling her often enough, she would start to believe that he really didn't mind and maybe he even enjoyed her company.

Chapter 15

Full dark had fallen a long time ago, and as Annie squinted out the window, she couldn't see anything but large trees on either side of the road. The ground didn't seem to be particularly steep, but she couldn't remember the last time they passed a house. Thirty minutes ago? Maybe more.

The kids, thankfully, had fallen asleep several hours previously, not long after they stopped for a bathroom break and to grab groceries and supper.

They hadn't waited to go to the store closest to the cabin, figuring that the kids would fall asleep since it was so late.

"You're getting sleepy?" Zeke murmured from the other side of the cab, sitting back behind the wheel and driving with confidence.

The remote area did not seem to bother him at all.

"Not really."

"Anxious?"

"That was your next guess?"

"I figure you must be feeling something. I'm just taking a stab in the dark, literally."

She smiled, because the darkness of the woods was a lot darker than regular darkness. If that made sense. Indiana was flat, with no deep woods like this, and of course, North Dakota barely had any trees at all.

"I'm just not used to darkness this thick," she said. "And being this remote. Are there any houses anywhere?"

"I didn't see too many on the map when I looked it up earlier today."

At the mention of earlier today, she smiled at the memories. "Are you warm?"

"It took me a little bit, but I feel like my feet have thawed out and I can feel my toes again. Mostly a nice feeling."

"No frostbite?"

"I might have to check tonight."

"Sorry about that."

"No apology necessary, I had fun. I think the kids did too, and I'm pretty sure you were smiling."

"I was." She hesitated, wondering whether she dared mention it, and then she said, "And I owe you something."

"I wasn't going to demand that I get paid if that wasn't something you wanted."

"Maybe we can talk about it later," she said and then wished she would have answered differently. She would like to have said, "yes, I would like to pay it," but the idea of kissing someone other than her husband...wasn't a terrible idea, it was just...new. New ideas weren't necessarily bad, just sometimes they took a little getting used to.

"Just a few more minutes, and we should be there."

"We don't have anything to do tonight, right?"

"It's chilly enough out that we might need to build a fire if it hasn't been done. But the animals are supposed to be taken care of for this evening."

"That's what I thought. But I'm tired enough that I probably ought to confirm, because I don't want something to go hungry because I was too sleepy to think about it."

"We're good. We just need to concentrate on the kids. I don't know exactly what the house is going to be, so not sure where we'll put them."

"Maybe one of us can walk in and check it out while the other one stays out here with them? That might be better than trying to carry a sleeping kid around, looking for a place to put them down."

"That sounds like a good idea," Zeke said as he turned the corner, and they saw lights in the distance.

Zeke looked at the map that was up on the screen on the console between them before he looked back out at the lights. "Looks like that's it."

"Wow. You can land an airplane out here."

"Maybe a helicopter. Unless they clear a lot more trees than what looks like they've taken out."

"Oh, that's right. I forgot. You actually couldn't land an airplane."

"Not here," Zeke said, looking around at the trees.

"Well, that's not exactly reassuring. How good are you with helicopters anyway?"

He grinned. "I think I could read the instruments, and I might be able to figure it out, but it would be something I would do only in an extreme emergency, like a flash flood."

She looked around. "If we run into a man with long white hair and a long beard, dressed in a robe, and talking about an ark, maybe we should start looking for a helicopter."

"Right. And if you run into that fella, maybe you are hallucinating a little bit more than what I was thinking to begin with. I'll just go ahead and take care of the animals myself."

She laughed.

Then lapsed into silence as the house came into view.

Annie felt her eyes opening wide. She'd never seen such grandeur. "I had no idea Elaine and her husband were so..."

"Rich?" Zeke supplied, irony in his voice.

"Yeah. Well. What, do they own a small country or something?"

"This looks like a palace anyway," he said. "By far the nicest place I've ever stayed." He huffed out a breath. "Maybe I should just sleep in the truck tonight. I feel like I'd walk in and just mess everything up."

"Yeah. And my kids. I'll need to tie them to chairs so they don't break anything expensive."

"They knew we were bringing children, and they said it was okay. I'm sure once we walk in, we'll figure out that there's someplace where we all can feel comfortable. Even if it is the basement. Or dungeon. Would a house like this have a dungeon?" Zeke asked.

Even though her anxiety had spiked rather than eased at seeing the house, his humor made her smile and forget that she was nervous. She'd never been so far out of civilization before. At least an hour to the nearest town, and almost that far to the neighbor's house.

"Do you want to go in and see if you can figure out where you want the kids? Or do you want me to do it?"

She looked around. "Do you think there's bears around?"

"Well, there probably are. But I'm betting that the bears around here see so few humans, they haven't figured out how to open up doors yet. So, even if you do see a bear, you don't have to worry about it from in the house."

She swallowed while Zeke smiled knowingly seeing that she was trying to be brave. "All right. And if they do figure out how to open the car door...I'll call you."

"Honk the horn. Maybe that will scare them away. I know it would wake the kids up, but I feel like it would be worth it."

"Me too." She could do that. Honking the horn might actually work. Unless it made the bear angry and he charged the pickup. She'd have to think about that. Maybe if the bear looked like it might get angry, she would wait to honk the horn until she was sure it was necessary.

By the time she figured that out, Zeke had gotten out and strode to the house.

There was an electric lock on the door, and he keyed in the number that they had been given, and it opened without any problems.

He looked in, switched the lights on, turned back around, and gave her a wave before he disappeared inside the house, closing the door behind him.

She went through some Bible verses in her head. Things about fear. The valley of the shadow of death seemed to be one that she was able to remember fairly easily, but she really didn't want to think about walking through the valley of the shadow of death right then, so she tried to think of another one.

What time I am afraid, I will trust in thee.

Surely God didn't bring her all the way out to this remote part of the world just to kill her.

Or just to let a bear eat her.

She had to have faith. Faith that God had a plan for her.

She started humming happy songs under her breath, which helped some, but it was a relief when she saw Zeke coming through the door again.

He walked over to her side of the pickup, and she wound the window down.

"I think it's not going to be too hard to get the boys in bed. When you walk up the stairs, which are to the right when you walk in, there's a room to the left at the top that has two single beds in them. The beds are made, and the place looks clean. So, if it's okay with you, we'll just go ahead and do that."

"I think that'll be perfect. If they wake up, we might want to take them to the bathroom. Did you notice where the bathroom was?"

"I saw there was a bathroom connected to that room. The door is between the two beds."

"Perfect," she said with relief.

"The dogs are barking, and you can really hear them when you walk in. I believe they said they were in cages in the mudroom off the kitchen at the back. They said once we got there, we could let them out. They're goldens and not aggressive at all."

"All right. I don't think the barking will wake the boys up, but if it does, it might be a good thing so the boys can go to the bathroom."

"Did you want a change of clothes for them or anything?"

"No. It's late, and we won't bother with anything like that. Their teeth aren't gonna fall out if we don't brush them one night."

"I'll take your word on that," Zeke said, and she had to grin.

"You didn't see any bears or anything, right?" she felt compelled to add.

"No. But you can go into the house first, and I'll get your back."

That was exactly what she wanted, and maybe it was dumb, but it made her feel so much better to know that she didn't have to look over her shoulder while she was walking in the house.

Maybe there weren't any bears within a hundred-mile radius of the house, but it felt like there was one standing behind every tree, just waiting for her to start walking up the walk before grabbing her from behind.

And if she were holding her child, she would have to fight for him too.

"I can see that eases your mind," he teased her as she wrinkled her nose at him and put her window up.

He walked around to the other side and carefully unbuckled Justin from his booster seat, while she went directly behind her and got Braden out.

Braden barely moved, settling into her arms when she had him released, while she could see Justin lifting his head up and blinking, looking around.

"We made it, buddy. Remember I told you we would be there tonight, but we're going right to bed."

"Where's Mommy?" Justin said, squinting at Zeke as though trying to figure out who he was.

"She's right there with your brother. He still asleep."

"Mom?" Justin said, peering over at her through the glow of the cargo light.

"I'm right here, honey. Trying to be quiet so I don't wake Braden up."

"I'm going back to bed?"

"Yes."

"I have to pee," Justin said, and she almost laughed at the wide-eyed look on his face.

"There's a bathroom upstairs. Just hold on."

Justin nodded, rubbing his eyes, before laying his head back down on Zeke's shoulder and allowing Zeke to adjust him so that he was able to carefully shut the door.

Zeke walked around to the front of the truck, and she heard him say, "If you leave the door open, we'll come back out and get our stuff and shut everything up."

"All right. That would be really helpful."

Braden snuggled in her arms, which made her smile at her sleepy warm little boy. And somehow, with Zeke's eyes on her, she didn't feel nearly as uncomfortable. Every once in a while, she could see him search the perimeter of the property, and it made her feel like he was taking her concerns seriously and not just going on the assumption that there were no bears and she was being silly.

Merle would have laughed at her fear and joked about it. And while she would have laughed with him, it wouldn't have made her feel better.

Zeke laughed with her, but he took her seriously as well. Which made all the difference.

She walked up the steps and was able to get the door open while continuing to hold Braden.

She felt like Zeke wanted to open the door for her, but he stood behind her like he said he would, standing sideways and keeping an eye out for her.

She made a mental note to thank him later. The fact that he wasn't just assuming that he was right and she was wrong did far more to ease her anxiety than anything else could have done.

"Up the stairs and to the left," Zeke reminded her, in case she had forgotten.

Or, more likely, because he might have known she was distracted by the grandeur of the house. Soaring ceilings, expensive-looking furniture, shiny mirrors, and large windows were the impression she got as she walked the few steps to the stairs and started up.

The whole stairs were open to the bottom, and as she rose, the place became even more impressive.

She did not feel like she belonged in a place this expensive. And she had no idea that Elaine and her husband had been so successful at...something.

Or maybe they'd inherited it. She wasn't sure.

"Straight ahead, then to the left," Zeke said softly behind her.

She'd been so busy looking at the house, she barely noticed the barking of the dogs, and she'd forgotten about Zeke behind her. She realized she heard him shut the door, and he was following her up.

She was glad he had given her directions, because although he told her how to find it, the house was very distracting.

She entered the room he indicated and saw the two beds just like he said.

Going to the right, because that was the bed closest to the door, she pulled the covers back and was able to lay Braden down without waking him.

He'd taken his shoes off in the truck, and she hadn't bothered to look for them before getting him out, so all that was left to do was arrange him and cover him up.

He was snoring softly when she straightened.

Zeke stopped behind her, holding Justin.

"Thanks," she said, taking her son from him.

He had been so gentle, so careful with the boy, it made her heart feel funny.

Funny in a good way, like he cared about her kids, and that made her happy.

Taking Justin, who was so much heavier than Braden, she went to the restroom.

"I think I'll be okay," she said softly in case Zeke wanted to go.

"All right. I'll watch the door and make sure no bears get in."

His eyes twinkled a bit, but his tone was serious, and she grinned, but her words were sincere. "Thank you."

Chapter 16

Zeke walked back down the stairs, smiling a little at Annie's obvious irrational fear of bears.

He could hardly imagine a bear coming out of the woods and attacking someone for no reason, but about the time he dismissed her for her fears, something might happen and he would feel terrible.

Still, it was kind of cute and made him feel like a protector to just make sure there were no bears in the yard.

He made a few trips in from his truck, carrying everything in but not taking it upstairs, since he wasn't sure where Annie wanted everything, then he moved to the kitchen, figuring out where the light switches were, and saw a piece of paper lying on the counter.

They looked like expensive countertops, maybe granite? He wasn't sure, but he figured it would take a while to get used to the opulence of the home. It was such a contrast to the remote, wooded location.

The paper contained instructions on the animals that needed to be fed and how to take care of the dogs.

Apparently there were also several cats and a litter box in the laundry room, wherever that was. He looked around the kitchen.

His eyes narrowed on the door that seemed to lead off to the side.

He walked over and opened it.

It was the pantry. Stocked full as he had been promised. He wasn't much of a cook, but he figured they could make plenty of meals out of the ingredients there.

The note said that they were to text any groceries they needed to the number at the bottom of the paper, and they would be delivered on Friday.

Moving down the wall, to the other side of the refrigerator, he opened another door. That was the laundry room.

Apparently there was a mudroom on the other side of the laundry room, and that was where the dogs were.

He walked through, and sure enough, they were in their cages, one on one side of the wall and one on the other.

The note said that the dogs would need to be walked the next morning and that they could be loose in the house as long as he and Annie were in with them. The note specifically requested the dogs be kept in their cages at night.

It also said there was an invisible fence around the yard and the dogs could be left out without leashes.

Speaking softly to the dogs, Zeke checked to make sure they seemed okay and then backed out of the room.

His disappearance set off more barking, and he felt bad that he'd bothered them, after they had settled down from them arriving earlier, but he didn't want to let them out and have them bother Annie while she was putting the boys down.

He walked back through the laundry room and into the kitchen. He had to admit he liked the house, felt a little pampered at the fanciness, and had enjoyed the ride here. Annie was a fun companion. She laughed at his jokes, for one, and was easygoing and not demanding. She was funny herself, and he had to admit he was looking forward to their time together.

Their silences had not been awkward.

He had just figured out the floodlights on the backside of the house when he heard footsteps on the stairs.

"Oh. You got everything carried in. That's great," she said as she reached the bottom.

"Yeah, if you let me know what room you're staying in, I'll carry the bags wherever you want. I assumed we weren't going to take the boys' stuff into their rooms until tomorrow morning."

"No. And I might even keep it in mine. We'll see. I did look around upstairs."

"There is a master bedroom downstairs. It has an attached bathroom, and it's pretty nice. But I wasn't sure whether you'd want that or not since the kids are upstairs."

"Yeah. I guess I would feel more comfortable if I were near them. So you go ahead and take that."

"I feel like that's a little bit too nice for me. I might just sleep on the couch."

Her brows went up in surprise, like she couldn't believe he would prefer a couch to the luxury of a king-size bed.

It wasn't really that he preferred it, he just...felt uncomfortable sleeping in someone else's bed.

"Well, I don't think I'm going to be quite that concerned. I'll pick whatever bedroom upstairs is near the boys." She looked at the paper on the counter. "Are those our instructions?"

"Yeah. I glanced over them and found the dogs, found the laundry room, and saw the litter box and the food. The dogs were in their cages, but I didn't see any cats."

"Sometimes cats are a little shy." She lifted a shoulder, like she wasn't going to worry about the cats for that night.

"You look pretty tired. Unless you want me to grab you something to eat or drink, I can carry your stuff upstairs."

"The animals outside? Are they okay?"

"Yeah, the note says that there are three mules, two cows, and a few goats. It says that there is a note out in the barn tacked up to the wall. So I figured I would check that out in the morning, since everything was supposed to be taken care of this evening."

"All right. Then I guess I'll grab my stuff and go upstairs."

"You can take your purse, just show me which bags to carry, and I'll take them up."

She pointed out three bags while she grabbed her purse.

He was able to carry two in one hand and one in the other, although none of them were heavy. He figured she had packed assuming that they would be able to use the washer and dryer.

He followed her up the stairs, and she poked her head into the door across the hall from her kids.

"This one looks fine," she said as she pushed the door open and turned the light on.

"I don't think there's an attached bathroom," he said, looking around the room.

"I think there's a bathroom at the end of the hall. That'll be fine."

"All right. Then you guys will stay up here and do all of your things, and I'll take the bedroom downstairs. I was going to sleep on the couch, but I think it might be better if I just keep my stuff and everything in that room."

He meant that they wouldn't be running into each other in various states of undress. Somehow, maybe because of the festival, or maybe just because he saw this more as a way to help Annie than anything else, the idea that they would be sharing a house together hadn't really sunk in.

It wasn't the type of thing he would normally do, but he'd been thinking about helping a friend, helping Annie, and hadn't considered all the ramifications.

Regardless, they were here now, and neither one of them were leaving, so he would make the best of it. Not that he minded being stuck at a house with Annie for a week.

Still, it seemed a little odd.

"Does anything seem off to you?" he asked.

Her eyes widened, and she froze, like his question was supposed to make her afraid.

"No. Not like that," he said, waving away her fear. "I mean the way people asked us to do this. Or the way this house is. Or... How well do you know the people who own it?"

"Elaine and I were friends, good friends back in the day. And she's married to Merle's cousin."

"Right. So you'd have a bit of a family connection."

"A very loose one. Why?"

"I guess I have a connection to Merle. He introduced me to his cousin, and we were all in the Air Force together. It's just..." He looked around the house. "This just says money to me. And that makes me feel like they could have hired someone to do what we're doing for the next week. I mean, they did hire someone, that person quit, but they could just hire someone else. They didn't need to rely on dubious family or friend connections. You know what I mean?"

He wasn't sure how else to explain it, but it just seemed odd that people who obviously had this much money would be relying on friends to house-sit for them.

"I guess I hadn't thought of that, but it is kind of odd. I hadn't talked to Elaine for years, and then all of a sudden, she's asking me to watch her house. But I guess I did suspect that maybe Mom was doing it to get me out of the house. She's been...on me about it."

He nodded, knowing she was a little sensitive to it and also knowing that she understood that there was a bit of a problem, but sometimes it wasn't easy to do the work necessary to fix the problem. He didn't want to push her.

"I guess that could be it, except that doesn't explain why I'm here."

"Well, it is pretty remote. I would be scared to death if you weren't here right now. I'm not sure I would have even gotten out of the car to walk to the house."

"Because of the bears?"

"So there *are* bears?" she said, like she'd just gotten him to admit something.

"No. I said that badly," he said with a little smile. But he did not laugh. "Not *the* bears, just bears. In case there are any."

"Yes. I don't know why I just look out there and I think bears. Behind every tree." She gave an exaggerated shiver, like she knew she was being unreasonable, and he laughed.

"I'd bet by the time we leave here, you'll be walking outside at night, unafraid."

"I hardly think so. I'm not even sure I'm going to go outside during the day."

"I think if there was anything dangerous, they would have said something. It's not like they sent us out here because they wanted to get rid of us. It just seems you being here doesn't really seem odd, but me? I haven't figured that out." He didn't mean to keep beating a dead horse, but he couldn't shake the feeling that something didn't add up. He just couldn't figure out what.

"You don't think it's enough that my mom wanted me to go, and she knew I wouldn't do it by myself?"

"Why didn't she go with you? Or why didn't she and some other woman from town. Or a retired guy from the church?"

Annie stood there for a minute, her finger tracing the edge of the dresser back and forth thoughtfully. "Do you think they were trying to set us up?"

"No. Not that. I can't imagine..." They were probably just trying to get Annie to come out of her shell. To snap out of the depression she was sinking into before it became a real problem.

"Maybe they weren't trying to set us up but just trying to put me with someone who makes me laugh. Mom commented that I was smiling more with you than with anyone."

Did she? He grinned. "Were you?"

"I wouldn't want you to get a big head about it."

"Oh, that's hardly likely to happen," he said, still smiling.

He liked the idea, not about getting set up, but that they thought he would be good for Annie. Interesting that he felt a pull toward her, and other people could see that maybe they would be good together too.

"I guess I can sleep on it. But that's all I can think of. I mean, I watched enough thrillers on TV that I could imagine us being sent here for other reasons, but I know my mom would never be a part of that."

"Yeah. Those kinds of things don't really happen in real life. I mean I guess they do but not to regular people."

She shook her head, as though shaking that thought off, and when she spoke, it was on a different subject. "All right. I suppose I'll work on cooking breakfast in the morning. Is there a certain time you want to eat?"

"Whenever you want to is fine. After I get done feeding the animals, I'll give you a hand with it."

"I'm pretty sure the cats and the dogs and the meals were my responsibility. I think we can each do our own laundry. And you'll take care of all the outside work, the cows and all the other animals along with the wood."

"Speaking of. I might build a fire, it's getting chilly."

"Do you need me to help you?" she asked, and he shook his head. She looked exhausted, and he'd feel better if she were upstairs sleeping.

"No. Not tonight. You look like you need to get some rest, and we'll figure the rest out in the morning."

She nodded and gave a little wave as she turned and walked toward her room

He watched her go. Maybe he shouldn't have, but he couldn't seem to pull his eyes away. There was something compelling about her that made him want to protect her and to get closer to her at the same time.

It might be an interesting week.

Chapter 17

Annie woke slowly, unsure at first where she was. Were those dogs barking?

She squinted at the clock beside the bed. Nine o'clock?

Were those her kids laughing?

She struggled to pull herself out from the deep sleep that she had been in since her head hit the pillow.

Slowly it came back to her. Yesterday had been a big day, with the festival and then the long drive, and then the house in the middle of nowhere.

And Zeke. He had been funny and sweet and helpful to her all day long. It had been one of the best days she could ever remember having. And her kids had enjoyed it too.

Her kids. She put her boys to bed in the bedroom right across the hall from her.

Throwing her legs out of her bed, she grabbed her clothes, hurried to change, and then ran to the bathroom.

By the time she was out, she was thinking that her boys should have woken up a long time ago, they should have come over to her, but maybe they hadn't realized where she was, maybe they had gone outside to look for her, maybe a bear had gotten them.

She gasped when she opened the bedroom door and both of their beds were empty and unmade.

Her heart beating fast, she ran downstairs, did a quick search of the kitchen and the open great room, and saw neither her boys nor Zeke.

She tried to calm herself. Had she heard laughing earlier?

Jogging across the room, she reached the front door where they'd come in the night before, and opened it.

She almost swallowed her heart as she saw Zeke and the boys playing in the yard. They had some kind of a ball, and they were all trying to kick it.

If there was any point to the game, she couldn't figure it out.

But she wanted to run out and tell them to get out of the yard, to come back inside, that there could be bears anywhere and they could all be eaten any second.

She managed to stop herself, step back in the house, and close the door. She walked to a window to continue watching them while she tried to get her heart rate and breathing under control.

Everything was fine. Her boys were fine, Zeke was fine, and there were no bears anywhere.

She hadn't realized she was so petrified of bears.

Or maybe it was just something that her mind had conjured up since driving through the deep woods, with no houses, no neighbors, no one to help if they needed it.

She was pretty sure that bears didn't typically walk out into a yard in the middle of the day and attack people.

She was being unreasonable. And she had almost yelled at Zeke over it.

But at least she didn't have to wonder whether or not she wanted to get out of bed this morning.

She almost laughed. That was one way to get herself up and not think about how miserable she felt.

In fact, all day yesterday she hadn't thought about how miserable she felt. There was a little bit of a cloud, but she was pretty sure there were actually times where she felt...okay.

She couldn't remember a time before that since Merle had died when the fog had completely lifted, the blackness had completely gone, and she felt like her old self.

Swallowing, taking another breath, she looked around for her shoes, putting them on before she walked, much more sedately this time, back out the front door.

She closed it behind her and walked to the edge of the steps.

Her movement caught Zeke's eyes, and he looked up. The ball hit his knee before he said, "Good morning!" His cheeks were red, and he was smiling, as were both of her boys.

They didn't notice that he stopped, and they continued to try to kick the ball.

"Are there some kind of rules to that game?"

"No. Just whoever can kick the ball does it."

"Oh. Okay. That's kind of what it looked like, but I thought maybe I was missing the bigger picture."

"No. You got it." Zeke grinned, then he looked at the boys. "Your mom's up. Run over and say good morning to her."

The boys didn't act like they wanted to, but they didn't complain either. Justin grabbed the ball, picking it up and putting it under his arm before he walked over beside Zeke.

Annie couldn't help but notice that he imitated Zeke's walk, the swing of his arm and the confidence there.

She hid a smile. It was too cute.

"I didn't mean to make you guys stop. I'll get started on breakfast if you all are hungry."

"I'm starved! Can we have pancakes?" Justin said, never one to turn down food.

"I saw the pantry last night, but I don't know what's in it."

"I looked, and there's a ton of stuff. I would almost bet there would be stuff to make pancakes in there."

She considered herself a fairly decent cook, and she could make them from scratch if she needed to, although a mix was always easier.

Regardless, she didn't go into the details with her boys, because they wouldn't care. They just wanted pancakes on their plate. So, she gave a time estimate just in case she had to make them from scratch and then said, "I'll text you when they're ready?"

"You'd better call. I might not hear it."

"Oh! I have to take care of the animals," she said as she realized the dogs were running around too, but she hadn't thought about it in her panic about what might happen to her boys.

"I've taken care of everything except for the cats. I haven't seen hide nor hair of them, and I'm kind of thinking that maybe they are make-believe."

"All right. You believe that, and I'll just go ahead and set the food out and see if something doesn't come and eat it."

"Like rats or mice or something." Zeke nodded. "Good idea."

She found herself laughing again as she turned away. Funny how he could do that. Just make her smile, coax a laugh out of her, even when she didn't want to.

"I'm leaving if I see any mice," she threw over her shoulder. "You might be staying here by yourself, because I don't share my house with rodents."

"All right. If I see one, I'm going to be sure not to tell you about it."

She laughed as she went in, toeing her shoes off and going to the pantry, where she found that Zeke's assessment was accurate. It had pretty much everything she could possibly want. Including all the ingredients to make pancakes.

She didn't see any pancake mix, but there were eggs and milk in the refrigerator and she got those out.

As she was putting the things on the counter, her phone rang.

It was Elaine.

"Hello?" she said, putting her phone on speaker so she could find a quick recipe for pancakes online.

"Annie, is everything good?"

"I think so. Zeke said he fed the animals this morning, and everything was good, although we haven't seen the cats."

"That's not too unusual. They're kind of shy. When I'm there, I don't usually see them until I sit down."

"All right. I'll keep that in mind. But otherwise, it's a gorgeous house. And somehow Zeke and the boys found a ball, and they've been playing in the yard."

"It was probably in the shed. There are baseballs and bats and a bunch of different things for kids to play with. I think there are even bikes you guys can use if you want to."

"Everything is so well-stocked. I feel spoiled."

Elaine laughed. "I'm glad I can spoil you a little. I appreciate you taking care of it. It's so remote that it is hard to find people who are willing to basically leave civilization to house-sit."

That reminded Annie, and she asked with a little bit of trepidation, "Do you see many bears?"

"No. Hardly ever. Why, did you see one?" Elaine asked, sounding surprised.

"No. I was just wondering."

"Oh. Sometimes things get into the trash if we forget to put the chain back over top of it, but we try to make sure to do that. Normally it's coons that we fight off though. Bears are few and far between, although we have seen them. Just not any lately."

"All right. That sounds good. I just... I've never been this far out before and I wasn't sure what to expect." She couldn't admit to her irrational fear, especially when it had been so unfounded.

"I love it there. The satellite internet works really well, and what else do you need?"

"I guess nothing. If they deliver groceries."

"Actually, they really don't. I have someone I paid to come up once a week. Every once in a while, I take a trip out, but my husband and I could just stay there forever. Although, I have to admit the Florida Keys are pretty nice too."

They talked a little bit about Elaine's vacation, and Annie had the pancakes mixed up with two cooking on the griddle by the time they hung up.

She dialed Zeke's number, letting him know that they were ready and they could come in at any time.

She smiled as she hung up. She had a feeling that this trip could be a life-changing experience. She couldn't exactly put her finger on why she thought that, but she hummed to herself as she hung up the phone and continued to make pancakes for her boys.

Chapter 18

Annie dried the last dish and put it away. The pancakes had been an unmitigated success. There hadn't been any left over, and Zeke had said twice how good they were.

She figured he probably wasn't used to someone cooking breakfast.

Of course, it had been a while since she had a man sitting across from her at the breakfast table. There was just something comforting in the fact that she was not alone.

"It's supposed to be pretty hot today. And there's a creek out back. I didn't know if you guys would like to go wading?" Zeke asked as the boys ran around the living room chasing the dogs.

The dogs had ended up being quite good with the kids, and Annie had relaxed as they had seemed to enjoy playing as much as kids did.

"That sounds like fun. My phone said that it was supposed to get chilly this evening and we might even have a storm."

"I saw that on mine, too. After we play in the creek and maybe have lunch, when the kids go down for a nap, I thought I'd go out and check on the store of firewood. It looks to me like the only form of heat is wood, so we'll probably want to make sure we have some to take the chill off."

"I can help you," she offered, unsure of exactly what she could do to help. "I've never run a chainsaw."

"I've done it a few times in my life, although I'd hardly call myself an expert. But it will definitely make it go faster, because you can carry what I cut, and we can probably get a good bit done while the boys are sleeping."

"Sounds like a plan," she said, reaching for the griddle and picking it up.

"Ouch," she said as the griddle clattered to the counter. She rubbed her shoulder.

"Are you okay?" Zeke took a step toward her, his brows furrowed, his face showing confusion.

And rightfully so, she really hadn't done anything worth getting concerned about.

"I must have pulled a muscle or twisted the wrong way or something. I just had a sharp pain in my shoulder."

She wiggled her fingers and moved her elbow, and everything was fine.

Then she moved her arm, and it was good until she tried to lift it over her head.

"Ugh. That hurts. Whatever it is, I'm good until I try to reach up."

"Probably nothing is broken. It might be a pull or strain. We can scratch everything we just said and take you down to an acute care facility."

"Oh my goodness. No. I don't need that. I'll just...probably just hurt for a little bit when I try to brush my hair, that's all."

"Well. It might keep you from carrying firewood, but it probably won't be anything serious."

"I agree. It will most likely feel better by tomorrow or the next day. In the meantime, I'll still try to do firewood, and I promise I didn't hurt myself on purpose just trying to get out of work."

"The thought never crossed my mind," he said, but then he winked and grinned at her, and she laughed.

They rounded up the kids, and they put on their sneakers. She figured that it would be better to have something on their feet, and she wasn't sure what the bottom of the creek would be like. It wasn't like she had waded around in mountain streams all of her life. In fact, she couldn't recall ever doing it. She'd dipped her tiptoes in Lake Michigan a few times and had been to Lake Erie once or twice as well. But she hadn't spent a lot of time in the woods.

"I always loved to play in water, no matter what kind of water it was, when I was a kid," Zeke said as they opened the door and the dogs ran out along with the kids.

"I guess I was a girly girl, and I didn't like to get wet or dirty. I spent a lot of my time inside, although I'm not sure exactly what all I did in there. I wasn't a big reader either."

"Well, it's never too late to start. You might find that you really enjoy it, and I'll have to drag you home for lunch."

"I hardly think that's gonna happen," she said, but while she wasn't exactly expecting to have a great time, she had realized that the more she got out and moved, the better she felt. At least that was the way it seemed yesterday, and she liked the fact that she wasn't thinking as much about the gloom and doom and that she was feeling better. She wanted to keep it that way, so whether it was movement or whether it wasn't, she was going to do things to keep her mind off where she didn't want it to go.

"You already lost one argument with me, are you sure you want to argue about this, too?"

She froze as the boys ran ahead, and they reached the edge of the yard.

She had forgotten all about the kiss she owed him. Although she didn't know how. It was kind of a big thing. And she found herself...almost looking forward to the idea. He'd been so much fun to be around, and she liked him.

Not that that surprised her, it just surprised her how much, and how the idea of kissing him actually seemed like something she might want to do.

He turned and looked at her, casually, like what he had said hadn't just rocked her world.

He tilted his head. "Did you forget?" he asked, like he couldn't believe that she would have forgotten.

"Is it terrible that I did?" She didn't want to say that she didn't find the idea terrible, either. Except... He wouldn't keep reminding her about it if he hadn't felt the same? Right?

"I'll have to make sure I pay you," she said finally, not able to get up enough nerve to tell him that it wouldn't be a hardship.

He did a slow grin that made her heart flip and her stomach twist. "I look forward to it."

Her eyes widened just a little. He'd said what she was afraid to.

"That's if we make it back from the creek alive," she said, needing to turn the subject to something else. She wasn't sure what was going on in her chest, but he seemed to be wearing down her defenses. Ones she hadn't even realized she had. And not with charm and flattery, but simply by being a man of character who also made her laugh and who was good with her children.

"And not get eaten by a bear?" he asked, and while he was teasing her, she didn't feel like he was making fun of her, but she felt like he was laughing with her, not at her. There was a difference, although she wasn't quite sure she could explain it.

"Well, as long as you don't get eaten by a bear," she said, emphasizing the "you."

"Me?"

"Why yes. After all, you're going to be running the slowest and letting the rest of us get away, right?"

"I suppose that has to do with the man's duty or something like that. Kind of how we're supposed to be the last ones off the ship. Ladies and children first?"

"Exactly. I'm so glad chivalry isn't dead."

"I don't know. I'll have to think on that one."

She laughed, knowing that he wasn't going to think about it at all. That he absolutely would make sure that they escaped before him if necessary.

"But I don't think we're going to meet any bears," she said with confidence.

"You don't?" he said, sounding surprised as they stepped into the cool shade of the woods.

The babbling of the brook could be heard over the chatter of the children.

He had told her that it wasn't very deep, so she wasn't worried about the kids, although she didn't want them to go out of her sight either. Thankfully the timber was mature and shaded the ground so that the briars and brambles couldn't grow.

"I don't. After all, you're not afraid, so why should I be?" And she realized that was true. Mostly. She had gotten a hold of herself earlier in the day, figured out that she did not need to go storming out to demand her way, and then as she watched, she realized that maybe she was being a little unreasonable and allowing fear to control her.

If she schooled her thoughts to think that the likelihood of the bear appearing, while they were making all that noise, and the dogs were barking and running around, was very low, and if she focused on the idea that they weren't far from the house, and more than likely nothing was going to happen, she found herself being cautious but not afraid. Not like it was when she focused on all the bad things that could happen and rolled them over and over in her head. Of course she would be afraid at that point.

"The invisible fence must run along the edge of the woods," Zeke commented.

"Oh. I didn't even realize the dogs stopped there. You're right." That would make their walk a little quieter and maybe make it less likely that one of her children would get knocked down in the creek.

"Hurry up, Mom!" Justin said, and she realized the boys had reached the edge of the water.

"They listen to you," Zeke said, not sounding exceptionally surprised but maybe pleased.

"Normally they do. And I certainly don't want them getting in the water without me."

She had told them at the breakfast table that she didn't want them going into the water without her.

"It's always worth the effort to train children," Zeke said casually.

"I agree. Although, sometimes it's an exhausting, thankless job."

"And you wonder if they're ever going to get it, yeah. And sometimes they are so rambunctious, they're not really being bad but just drive you crazy anyway."

"So true. Boys. I think that's the way they are."

He laughed and couldn't disagree.

"Can we go in now?" Justin asked as Zeke and Annie reached the bank of the water.

The woods were not steep, and the water flowed down bubbling over rocks and trickling through pebbles. There was a spot where it was a little calmer and looked to be about knee-deep. Annie saw fish darting through the shadows in that area.

"Do you think there are snakes here?" she asked, looking at the creek and honestly not sure.

"There might be. But I think they are probably like bears. As long as they hear us, see us, or sense us, they're going to leave us alone. Animals don't usually challenge humans, unless they have babies."

"Or grizzly bears. They'll attack for no reason."

"That's true. I've heard that. But I don't think that's something we have to worry about here."

"You're right. I guess I just wanted to point out that there are exceptions to what you said."

"Okay. You could also point out that lions, tigers, and sharks are an exception as well."

She laughed, getting his meaning. It was hardly an exception if it was something that they didn't have to worry about.

"All right. Thank you for pointing that out. Boys, keep an eye out for sharks." She nodded her head. "Otherwise, feel free to go in the water. Do not go out of my sight."

"Yes, ma'am," Justin said, turning and splashing into the water. No tiptoes for that kid.

Annie had to laugh because Justin had such a big personality.

Braden was a little slower, but after his initial squealing when the cold water seeped through his sneakers, he splashed around with his brother.

Zeke plowed into the water with them, splashing and laughing, and helping them build a dam.

Annie moved upstream just a little, close enough she could still see and hear them, but far enough away that she wasn't going to get wet anywhere she didn't choose to.

She stepped carefully into the water, biting back a squeal that would have sounded an awful lot like Braden's as the cold water hit her toes. She hadn't been expecting it to be so chilly.

But it was invigorating too, and she loved watching it as it shimmered and flowed, bubbled and gurgled. The sunlight shimmered over the tops as the wind rustled the leaves and created dancing shadows on the water. In some places, she could see straight down to the little pebbles at the bottom, and in others, the water flowed too fast or the shade made it murky.

She could see why Zeke had said water fascinated him as a child. She could see her younger self being fascinated as well. Her older self was fascinated. She'd never taken the time to appreciate the ever-changing flow of water over rocks.

"Mom! Come down and play with us!" Justin called, stomping through the creek and throwing up big droplets of water everywhere as he came toward her.

She wanted to reprimand him, to tell him to slow down, to not get her wet, and then she realized how silly that was. If she didn't want to get wet, she shouldn't be standing in the water.

Still, it wouldn't hurt for her son to learn to be considerate either. Before she could open her mouth though, Zeke said, "Hey, kid, take it easy. Don't splash your mom if she doesn't want to get wet."

"Huh?" Justin said, turning around and looking at Zeke like he'd suggested Justin should fly to her instead of walk.

"Sometimes people don't want to get splashed, and the way you're walking is throwing water up, which will splash your mom."

"Oh." Justin still looked a little confused,

Zeke said, "Just walk a little slower so you're not throwing water up with your feet or making big splashes when you walk."

"Oh. Okay," Justin said, lifting one foot out of the water and setting it back down in, then lifting another foot out and setting that back in, and taking great big strides as he continued toward Annie.

"Mr. Zeke is right. You're being a lot more considerate now. But we also have to consider that people shouldn't be in the water if they don't expect to get wet."

Justin, concentrating on his careful walking, barely nodded at her.

"I see fish!" Braden called from where he had stayed down at the slow, deeper part of the creek.

"Can we catch some?" Braden asked, looking up at Zeke.

Zeke murmured something that Annie couldn't hear over the water, and for the next couple of hours, they built dams, tried to catch fish unsuccessfully, found a couple of crawfish, and once Zeke touched her arm gently, pointing out the silver flash of a snake as it slithered on downstream.

That, Annie could live without seeing, but there was still something fascinatingly beautiful about it, and she appreciated Zeke seeing it and showing her.

It also made her wonder if that creature had any friends that she hadn't met yet, but she didn't dwell on that thought either. After all, they had played for several hours and not seen anything. She wasn't going to let a glimpse of one spoil all of her fun.

Soaking wet and shivering, they dragged themselves out of the creek long after lunchtime, laughing and talking as they did so.

She couldn't believe the boys weren't exhausted, but there was something about the cold water that was invigorating.

She suspected they would sleep like logs all afternoon.

The boys skipped ahead, starving and ready to eat.

She and Zeke followed more slowly.

"Thanks for suggesting this. This was a lot of fun." She had to admit she had been happy all morning. Without even thinking about it. She couldn't figure out whether it was Zeke, or the mountain, the exercise, or a combination of everything. Maybe even the new environment.

"I'm glad you came. I definitely had a good time with you and appreciated you being such a good sport. I suspect this is not something you would have chosen to do had you been given a choice."

"No. I probably would have chosen to stay in the house and sit around. I'm glad I didn't. This was a new experience and one I hope to repeat."

"We can certainly come here again. Although, I think tomorrow is supposed to be pretty chilly."

"Yeah, there's that storm tonight. Do you think that the creek will...flood or anything?"

"Most likely not. I think it's far enough away from the house and downhill that we don't have to worry about it. We'd have to get an awful lot of rain for it to get that high."

"I didn't realize that it was a slope on the way down, but I'm a little out of breath climbing up the hill now."

"I can push you if you need me to," Zeke said.

"Show-off," she said, which made him fall back, put his hands on the small of her back, and push.

"Actually, that helps."

He laughed, and pushed her for a few more steps, then fell back into step beside her.

"How's your arm?" he asked as the dogs barked at them as the boys reached the edge of the yard.

"I actually forgot about it. As long as I don't put it up over my head, it doesn't hurt."

As though she had to try it out, she lifted her arm, and as it got about shoulder high, it started to hurt.

She let it drop back down and did not mean to have her hand brush Zeke's.

But it did, and she wasn't sure exactly how it happened, but after the first brush there was a second one, and their fingers slid together, and a second later, they were walking with their hands clasped between them.

It felt natural and right, and she didn't want to pull her hand away, even though she thought that maybe she should.

After all, it was kind of her fault. Since she had been the one to raise her arm.

"Hey," he said, squeezing her hand.

She took a breath and then looked up at him. "Yeah?"

"If you want to hold my hand, just say so. You don't have to do that whole sneak attack thing."

She said, "Oh!" and tried to yank her hand away, but he clasped it tight, chuckling at her feigned annoyance.

"I'm teasing. I like it. And I was the one who snagged your fingers. Although you were the one who touched me first."

"I'm sorry. I...don't want it to mean more than what it does." She wasn't sure exactly what she was saying with that, but just maybe that as natural as it felt, and as perfect, she wasn't sure what she was saying with it.

"It doesn't have to mean anything more than what you want it to," he said. And his words were serious. Reassuring her. But then he added with a small grin, "Although it doesn't count for the kiss that you owe me. Just so we're clear on that."

"Oh my goodness. You are never going to let it go, are you?"

"Not with you. I suppose, if it were someone else, I might be walking around hoping they forgot about it, but yeah. I'm not doing that."

That was the second hint he had given that it might be something he was looking forward to. A little voice told her to go ahead and admit that she was looking forward to it too, but she just couldn't bring herself to say. So, she smiled, squeezed his hand, and continued walking into the yard. There would be plenty of time to tell him some other time.

And then she stopped that line of thinking in its tracks.

She, if anyone, knew that there wasn't always plenty of time to say what needed to be said. Or what one should say. She shouldn't allow time to go by without saying the things that should be said. Because one never knew when the people one loved would be called home.

"I'm looking forward to it too."

Chapter 19

Zeke wanted to stop short and drag her into his arms immediately.

It was an odd sensation. He couldn't remember the last time he had wanted to get closer to someone so fervently.

Maybe it was because she was all wet and looked cold, and he wanted to warm her up. But he knew that wasn't the slightest bit true. It had nothing to do with how cold she was, or even the fact that he wouldn't mind getting a little warmer either. Although he figured if they were going to do wood later, he'd get warm soon enough.

That wasn't the issue.

He'd had such a good time. In truth, he'd enjoyed playing with the kids, but he didn't think that he would love spending hours in the creek with just two little boys, if their mom hadn't been with them.

She definitely made it so that he had forgotten everything, the time, how cold he was, and even the fact that they were supposed to be watching someone else's house.

He should make sure everything was ready for the storm. Not just making sure that they had wood, but that the animals were taken care of, and try to figure out what the backup would be if the electricity went out.

With the temperature drop, he had a wind advisory on his phone, and he figured that the elevation was high enough that they could actually get some serious wind.

But he hadn't been thinking about any of that this afternoon. Just about Annie, and how cute she was, how much fun, how much he enjoyed teasing her and laughing with her and talking to her. How, once she got out of the depression she'd been in, she was exactly the kind of woman that he could see himself settling down with.

Other than she seemed like she was a city girl, and he had already made a life for himself on the farm. He didn't want to have to give that up.

The kids ran into the house, taking their shoes off and making sure that they were dry enough that they weren't going to leave tracks through the house.

Sitting them down at the table, he and Annie worked together to make sandwiches and get them drinks.

Lunch was quiet, and it was obvious that the boys were exhausted from the hours they spent playing.

It was a good exhaustion, and the boys had a healthy glow about them.

The quietness of the dinner table was a huge difference from the noise of splashing and laughing in the creek, but Zeke loved both aspects of family life. The happy fun times together, and the quiet, easy silences between them.

Taking the boys upstairs, he helped Annie change their clothes, and they tucked them in for a nap.

Annie softly closed their door, and they tiptoed down the stairs.

"I'm pretty sure they're going to be sleeping for a really long time."

"That's good. We can spend a good two hours doing wood, then maybe we can come in and take a break before they wake up for the evening."

"That sounds good to me," Annie said, biting her lip. "You're going to have to tell me what to do though. I've...never cut wood in my life before."

"It's just a matter of cutting it and then stacking it somewhere. Stacking it is pretty intuitive, but I can show you what needs to be done." He eyed her, trying to figure out if she was the kind of person who would work no matter what, or whether she'd be honest about her pain. "If your arm hurts you, you're going to tell me, right?"

She smiled a little and ducked her head. Like she was guilty.

That's kind of what he thought. She would feel like if she wasn't helping, she wasn't pulling her weight, and so she wouldn't tell him if it hurt.

"I'm going to ask you, and I expect an honest answer, okay?"

"I can promise you an honest answer," she said easily, and he believed that. She didn't seem like the kind of person who would lie, even to tell what the world considered little white lies to grease social interactions. That eased his heart. Lies, even "little" ones that served to grease social interactions, could come back to bite a person. And God didn't make any exceptions for any kind of lying. It was all an abomination to Him.

"All right, I saw a chainsaw in the shed this morning when I was looking around at things."

"You must have gotten up really early," she said as she stuck a pair of boots on and walked out the door he held open for her.

"I usually wake up pretty early. And I'm not very good at just lying around in bed. Once I'm awake, I want to be doing something."

"I'm probably the opposite. I could lie in bed for hours after I wake up. Quite happily. If my kids would let me. Which they typically don't, and this morning, I was a little panicked when I didn't hear or see them."

"I'm sorry about that. I knew I should let you know what I was doing, but I didn't want to send you a text, because I was afraid that would wake you up. And I figured after the big day you'd had yesterday, that you could use a little extra sleep."

"I appreciate the consideration. And I'll try to keep that in mind tomorrow morning if I don't hear my kids when I wake up."

"You can assume that if I'm capable of it, I'm watching them." He put a hand on the shed door and paused to look at her. "Does that ease your mind?"

"It does. Although I think I already knew that."

"You wouldn't be a good mom if you weren't concerned about your children." He meant it as a compliment. Just watching her with her kids had shown him that even though maybe she wasn't in a great place mentally, whatever was best for her children came first to her. He saw her pushing herself to do things that maybe she didn't want to just because it was best for her kids.

He thought in the process of doing that, she had ended up feeling better herself.

"Here's the chainsaw I thought we had. When I talked to Brett, he said there was one out back, but they used up almost everything that was cut and split." He reached for the chainsaw and set it on a low wooden bench.

"I'm gonna check the fuel before we go out." He spoke as he unscrewed the cap for where the mixture of gas and oil went.

"Glad I did. It's empty," he said as he jiggled it, not seeing any liquid at all at the bottom. "It looks like they had run out of gas and decided to quit at that moment."

Looking around, he saw a can that had "chainsaw oil" written on it. Typically, chainsaws ran on a mixture of gas and oil, and he figured the stuff in that container was already mixed up. But when he picked it up, it was empty.

"I think I might know why they had used up all the wood they had and didn't have anything more cut."

"We're completely out?" Annie said, sounding a little concerned.

"I'll keep looking around, but I don't see anything else. We can mix up gas and oil for fuel, and I see a couple of bottles of oil right there on the shelf." He walked over and picked them up. They were full, unopened. "But I don't see any gas."

His gaze swept the shed again, confirming his suspicion.

"I'm going to have to run down to town and grab some. My phone said it was going to be in the forties, and the only heat for the house is wood. I don't think you're going to want to go without it, since that's going to be the high tomorrow."

"No. That sounds...like the best thing to do."

He heard the concern in her voice and stopped. In his mind, he was already figuring out the steps of what he needed to do, go get gas, come back up, cut wood, make sure it didn't need to be split, and split it if it did. Do enough to have a fire for his family for at least a day. Wait. Not his family. For Annie and her boys. They weren't his family.

Odd that his brain was going in that direction, and he thought that with no deliberate thought.

But he hadn't considered that Annie might not want to be left up here alone. She wasn't used to being so secluded nor used to being so far out.

"Annie? If you don't want me to leave you, we can wait until the boys wake up."

"We're supposed to get a storm tonight. It would be better for you to go down the mountain and be back up here before the storm than for us to wait until the boys woke up and drive in it."

He couldn't disagree with that, but she didn't look very happy about it.

He took another step to her and put his hand on her shoulder. He teased her earlier about holding his hand, but after her original mock outrage, she hadn't tried to pull her hand away. She also hadn't protested about the kiss he kept reminding her about... She said she was looking forward to it.

He wasn't sure what was happening between them, but he knew he felt protective toward her in a way that he hadn't felt toward anyone else. He also wanted to make sure that whatever he did pleased her. Which was another odd sensation. He cared, truly cared, about what she wanted and what made her happy. He found himself doing things just to make her smile. It wasn't necessarily a bad thing, just...said that maybe his feelings were starting to run a little deeper than just liking Annie as a friend.

"I'll stay if that's what you want."

"No."

"I don't want you up here by yourself, scared."

"I'm a little bit concerned, I'm not used to being in the middle of nowhere with no one close by. But there is good cell service, and you'll most likely be back before dark."

"Almost certainly. It's only an hour down and an hour back. I should be home by suppertime."

"You'll still have all the animals to do when you get back."

"That will be fine. They'll be okay."

"And so will we. Why don't you go ahead and get going, that way you get back faster." She lifted her chin and met his gaze with a bold one of her own.

He liked that she was jutting her chin out and was determined to not be scared. "Annie?"

"Yeah?"

He didn't know what he wanted to say. Ask for his kiss? Yeah. He would like that. But he didn't really want to kiss her, then leave. He'd rather have a hello kiss.

"Call me if you need anything, okay?"

She pulled both lips in her mouth, and then one of her hands came up and settled on his side, right above his hip.

He could feel the burning under his T-shirt.

"I will."

Maybe it was her hand on his side, or maybe it was the fact that she let him hold her hand, but he didn't quite do what he wanted to do. He put his arms around her and drew her into his chest.

"You're going to be just fine," he said, putting his cheek on the top of her head and feeling her arms come around his waist.

"I know. Maybe, maybe when you get back, or after we put the kids to bed tonight, I can pay what I owe you."

"I don't want you to pay because you owe me. But if you want to do it just because you want to, I'm down for that."

She laughed a little but didn't say anything.

He held her for just a few minutes, and she felt soft and warm and good in his arms, and the last thing he wanted to do was pull away and get in his truck and drive down the mountain, but it's what he needed to do. And she was right, the sooner he did it, the better.

So he pulled back and stepped away until he was holding onto her shoulders again with both hands, an arm's length between them.

"You go on in the house, and do me a favor."

"What?"

"Stay inside until I get back, okay?"

"You do not have to ask me to do that twice." She grinned, like she found it a little funny, but that she was going to be staying inside anyway.

"All right, I'm going to grab the gas cans, throw them in the back of my pickup, and head out. You call me if you need anything, and I'll let you know if anything comes up with me. Although I'm not expecting anything to," he added, just so she wouldn't think that he was thinking that there was going to be some kind of problem. He wasn't, but he wanted her to know that he would be in touch.

"All right. You be safe."

She seemed like she didn't want to move, but then she kind of shook herself and turned, walking out of the shed and hurrying into the house.

He watched her until she disappeared, and then he reached down and got a gas can.

Maybe, once he figured out what kind of stores were in town, he'd text her and see if she wanted him to pick anything up. Since it took so long to get to town, they probably weren't going to be making very many trips, and he didn't want her to run low on anything.

Smiling, because there he was again, caring about Annie and wanting her to be happy, he whistled a little as he walked toward his pickup.

Chapter 20

"If you help him, smile at him, don't get upset about silly things. And of course, *of course*, he should reciprocate, but if he doesn't, realize that contrary to what the world tells you, that it's an abusive relationship or whatever, you don't always have relationships that are completely equal. And, if you want to keep your balance, you have to do your best. And trust that God will reward you."

June held the hand of Verna who sat beside her in the back pew of the empty church.

They had agreed to meet here because it was private and was also a calming place for both of them.

"I'll try to remember. Do you have a list of verses?" Verna asked, looking at her Bible like she might have stuck them in.

"Here. Take my list. I have another one at home," June said, handing her a list of verses that they had gone through when they had started.

"Thank you so much. If you hadn't been willing to meet with me these last few weeks, I don't think my husband and I would still be married. And, I want so badly to have a solid home for my children."

"I'm so pleased that you are thinking of your children. That shows maturity that most people don't have," June said sincerely. She couldn't help but think of the irony of her helping people with their marriages, when her marriage seemed to be nothing but a sham. At least on her husband's end.

She wondered what they would say if she told him that her husband cheated and she had been thinking about leaving. That didn't make her advice any less valid, but it did make her example... At least in her eyes it made her an example less.

"Thank you again for your time," Verna said as she stood.

June stood with her, and walked her to the vestibule door.

"I think I'm going to stay here and pray for a bit," June said as Verna put a hand on the door.

"If I need more help will you be okay if I keep calling you?"

"Any time. Day or night. Please." June had already fielded some late night/early morning calls from Verna. And she certainly didn't mind. Sometimes a person just needed a comforting voice to talk to, someone to remind them of why they were doing what they were doing. To help them let go of the anger and remember the path they had chosen to walk. It was a hard path, sometimes even June wanted to take a break.

"Thanks again," Verna said, giving her a short hug and then hurrying out.

June said a short prayer while she was walking back to the pew that Verna's marriage would be restored.

Her husband had seemed to be coming around as Verna had started making the effort to be kind, even when he wasn't. For most people, it was difficult to be unkind to someone who was being kind to them.

June's husband was an exception, but that was how narcissists were. They did a lot of taking and precious little giving.

June sat back down on the pew, praying again that God would give her direction in her own marriage. She wasn't quite sure how she'd started counseling several young women in their marriages, but the pastor had recommended her, and she'd done her best.

Whether the pastor realized what was going on in her own marriage, she didn't know. At least he knew that her husband didn't attend church, and the fact that he wasn't a regular attendee didn't disqualify her from being able to counsel others had surprised her.

Maybe he figured she knew the pain of being alone, yet still married. It was a deeper aloneness, one that couldn't be assuaged, one that had no hope. At least a person who was single had the hope of someday meeting someone and having a lifetime partner to share their joys and sorrows with.

For her, she was just facing a lifetime of being alone. With her husband uninterested in being with her, and the vows that she had said to him prohibiting her from finding someone else.

Unless she divorced him.

The temptation was always strong, always something in her mind that she couldn't quite push away. God had been strangely silent on the subject. Other than telling her to wait, that He would fight for her, beyond that, she hadn't had clear direction, and so she'd been sitting still, waiting.

She moved on to prayer for her friends and acquaintances when her phone rang.

Digging in her purse, she pulled it out and swiped.

"Hello?"

"June. It's your realtor, Cindy. I have a house I think is perfect for you. It checks all of your boxes. Would you like to see it?"

Lord?

"Hello? Are you still there?" Cindy said, with that excitement that realtors often were able to infuse into their voices.

"Sure." June didn't have anything planned, and one of her boxes was that the house had to be within a ten or fifteen minute drive of Sweet Water. So, she knew it wouldn't be taking long, and should be back in plenty of time to get some supper cooked before Wayne got home.

"All right. I'll text you the address, and I'll meet you there in... twenty minutes? Will that be okay?" Cindy must have been texting as she talked because June's phone buzzed with a text as Cindy asked about the time.

"Sure. That'll be fine."

"All right. Let me know if you have any trouble. Otherwise, I've already told the owners that I was going to be showing it this afternoon."

"Wow. You have a lot of confidence in me."

"I'm telling you, you're going to love it!"

June smiled, figuring that she would see for herself how she felt about the house and she promised to meet Cindy before they hung up.

She stood up, clicking the link on her phone, and scrolling down through as the house loaded.

It was small, two bedrooms, which was one of her requests, with a fenced yard, that would be perfect in case her cats slipped through the door, although they didn't usually run out. Still, she also wanted a fenced yard just in case she decided to get a dog.

The kitchen was nice, spacious, with an island and granite countertops.

She hadn't wanted a whole lot of extras, but she definitely appreciated the upgrades.

Most importantly, it was close enough to town for her to feel like she wasn't isolated, but far enough away that she would have some privacy.

She met Cindy at the drive, both of them being five minutes early. After they greeted each other, Cindy invited her to walk around the yard and then unlocked the door and they stepped in.

Cindy talked about the assets of the house, while June followed along, pointing out something here or there, but for the most part just listening.

If felt a little bit like home. But it also felt scary. The idea of buying a home without her husband. She hadn't expected to be at her age, and to be shopping for a home by herself. She definitely hadn't expected to be shopping for a home and thinking she was going to leave the one she was living in to her husband.

But she didn't want to fight, didn't want to have a bunch of lawyers involved, didn't want to take anything her husband didn't think she deserved, and she suspected that he probably didn't think she deserved anything.

By the time they'd gone through the two bedrooms upstairs, and come back down to the living room with the gas log fireplace and the big picture window that overlooked the fields behind the house, she decided that even though it was scary, maybe she'd make an offer.

Her online business had been doing fairly well, and she had money for a down payment. She'd seen the price when she looked at the listing, and it was right in her price range. Maybe just a little bit more than she was comfortable spending, but not more than what she could.

"How do you feel about it?" Cindy asked, as they stood in the living room and looked out the big picture window.

"I love it. You're right. It checks all of my boxes. And it's perfect."

"I'd love to be able to tell them that they can expect an offer from you."

"I'd love for you to be able to do that too, but I think I need to pray about it a little bit."

Cindy's face fell, but not by much. "It's a hot market, and this is priced below market value. It's not going to last long."

"I'll keep that in mind." June didn't bother to tell her that if it was the Lord's will for her to get the house, it would last as long as she needed it to in order for her to believe that God wanted her to have it.

She stood in the living room, thinking, considering things she'd never considered before. If she bought this house, she would be mowing the grass. She always mowed the grass before, but she would have to buy a lawn mower. She had never done that. She just used whatever her husband had provided.

If there was anything she needed fixed, she would have to do it. Of course, she could call her kids. Either one of her boys would be happy to come help her. And, hadn't she been fixing her own things for years?

The leaky faucet that she asked her husband to fix and he hadn't, she had finally watched YouTube videos and fixed it herself.

She'd always done the maintenance around her house. She could do it here, too.

It was just a big step and...scary

Lord, I'll take this step if it's your will, but I need to be sure that this is what you want. I... don't want to do this without you. I can do it without my husband, but I'm not going to do it without you.

"Thanks so much for showing it to me," she said to Cindy, turning toward the door and waiting for Cindy to open it.

"I'll be sure to give you a call, but you're right. It's absolutely perfect for me, but I just want to make sure I talk to a few people before I go jumping in."

"I totally understand. Buying a house is a major decision, and you don't want to do it on the spur of the moment. But, at the same time, you don't want to wait too long, because like I said, this is a hot market and this house is not going to last long."

"I'll keep that in mind."

And she would. She would move just as soon as she was sure it was God's will.

Chapter 21

Annie walked around the house, trying not to think about looking at her watch, yet again.

The wind had kicked up, and it gusted with frightening force at times.

It was like she'd never been home alone before even though she'd spent almost an entire year alone after Merle's death. But that was a little different. First of all, she was in the neighborhood she was familiar with, she could look out any window of her house and see another house. Another neighbor. Someone who could help her if she needed it.

She could look out her front door and see a street that almost always had a car or several on it.

Someone to stop and help her if she needed it.

And she could call 911 and the police would be there...soon. As soon as they could be.

She hadn't realized how much she had depended on those security blankets in order to feel safe.

Wasn't she supposed to depend on the Lord? And she would have said that she did. Except, without the security of police and neighbors and even strangers on the street to help her, she was scared. It showed her just how little faith she had in God and how much she had in man.

She had it all backward.

Swallowing hard, she walked from the kitchen to the great room, looking out the huge two-story windows at the yard and the trees surrounding it.

The wind whipped them back and forth, the whites of the leaves showing and several of them bowing with the force of it.

She wasn't exactly scared...never mind. She was petrified. And it had only been an hour and a half. At the very least, it would be two hours before he got back. That was if he went right down and came right back, with no issues at all.

She assumed there was a gas station at the town they had said was an hour away. That was assuming he found the town okay, the gas station was open, and he was able to get what he needed and come right back.

Her phone rang, and it startled her. She grabbed it, thinking that maybe it was Zeke and something happened.

Glancing at it before she swiped, she realized it was her mother.

A familiar voice would be very welcome, but she tried to school her emotions. She didn't want her mom to know exactly how upset she was. It wouldn't do to have her worried. After all, she had mostly good news to tell her mom. She felt good, with no sad or dark times all day. Until Zeke had left.

She couldn't really count fear as a depression-like symptom though. She was simply afraid because she wasn't used to being alone and didn't want to be. Because she hadn't been trusting God with her safety.

"Hello?" she said, pleased with how her voice sounded.

"Annie. I got your text last night saying you got there okay, but I thought I'd give you a call and see how today went."

Her mom sounded normal. Cheerful, relaxed, and happy.

"It's okay, Mom. You could admit you missed us."

"Well, honestly the house is quiet. And... I do. I don't think I've ever said that I look forward to you leaving, but I don't want you to stay when you have opportunities like this."

"You should see the house, Mom. It's amazing. I've never seen a place like this, let alone stayed in one."

"It's that nice?"

"It sure is." She went into a description of the house, turning away from the window so she wouldn't continue to see how the wind was blowing. Although she could hear it rattle the windowpanes.

"The kitchen sounds like a dream," her mom said five minutes later when she finally stopped gushing about what an amazing house it was.

"It is. And I haven't actually been out to the stable yet, but Zeke said there were a couple of cows and some mules and a few goats. I guess I saw a couple of them penned up just beyond the yard."

She walked over to the great room window again. She could see the fence, but the animals weren't outside. They were probably smart to be finding shelter somewhere.

"We played in the creek today. Mom, I was in the creek."

"You're kidding. Like, you got wet in the creek?" Her mom couldn't believe it. And rightfully so, she was such a girly girl.

"Yes. I got wet from head to toe. And I was going to chop firewood too, except the chainsaw was out of gas, and Zeke had to go to town to get the gas can filled up."

"So he's not there?" her mom asked casually, like it wasn't a big deal for her to be alone in the woods by herself without him.

"No. He should be back in another half an hour or so."

"My goodness, Annie. I'm so proud of you. I would have thought that you would have answered the phone saying how scared you were."

"I can admit to being a little bit frightened. It's so weird to be here by myself, I mean, it is really the middle of nowhere."

"How have you been...feeling?" her mom asked, sounding hesitant for the first time.

Annie knew her mom couldn't see her, but she smiled big. "Would you believe that I don't even know what it is, maybe the fresh air, just being active, being out? I'm not sure, maybe it was just a change of scenery, but I've felt...really good all day." Unless one counted the time after Zeke left, but she didn't mention that since it didn't really count.

"I'm so happy to hear that!" her mom said, and her tone mirrored her words.

Annie was sure that her mom was truly happy.

No one had been a bigger champion for her than her mom.

"I'm so glad you went. I was afraid you would turn it down, and I was really hoping that that would get you out of whatever hole you'd fallen into."

"I know you care about me, Mom. And I do think this is a really good idea. I can't even find it in myself to be upset that you kind of manipulated me into it."

"Just a little bit. Maybe," her mom said, and there was a smile in her voice. But Annie had been sincere; she wasn't going to be upset with her mom for pushing her in this direction. Maybe, just maybe she could admit that her mom had been right. That she just needed to suck it up and be active, go do something, and get her mind off herself.

She knew from experience that that wouldn't solve depression in everyone, but it worked for her. She wished she would have tried it sooner.

"I need to talk to Zeke, but he mentioned that there were jobs at the farm. I... I might be getting one."

"Zeke is a really great guy," her mom said, and she had to agree. But it sounded like her mom was implying more.

"What are you saying, Mom?"

"I saw you guys at the festival yesterday. I know you didn't see me, because you were so busy laughing with him."

"You're right. I thought you were in the kitchen all day."

"I got to get out and take a walk around a little bit. I was going to come and take the kids off your hands for a bit, but you and he were having such a great time, I didn't want to go over and interrupt you. I love seeing you smiling."

"I had a really great time. I actually felt really good yesterday too."

"It looked like it," her mom said simply.

"You know, Mom, I should get on you the way you've been on me. I'll have you married by the end of the year."

"Let's get you settled first, and then we'll worry about me. I'm actually pretty happy in my house with my accounting business and my friends in town. I'm not sure I want to do the whole marriage thing again."

That made Annie a little bit sad. "You know, Mom, I said the same thing. But I think I might be changing my mind."

"You're a lot younger than I am. You have a lot more life ahead of you. Plus, your boys need a dad."

"I don't want to pick just anyone for their dad. Just because you marry someone doesn't automatically make him a dad to your kids."

"And that's the truth."

Her mom hadn't gotten married again, and in later years, she'd confessed that was part of the reason. She just had never found a man who would treat her kids the way he treated his own. There was no point in getting married and trying to combine families if it just never worked out.

It was a joining that was hard to accomplish and often created a lot of problems for second marriages.

Her mom hadn't wanted that, had thought that she would be better off without it.

Annie couldn't say for sure whether her mom was right or not, but she appreciated her mom always thinking of her and putting her needs first. She hoped she was that good with her own children.

"Oh. I forgot to tell you. A farmer down by Rockerton got caught in his baler. He lost a leg and almost lost his life. He was life-flighted to the Cities. They are having a fund drive for his wife. Maybe you can give me a hand with that when you get back."

"Of course," Annie said without needing to think about it. But the idea of the woman who could lose her husband struck her hard. Even if this was a farmer and not a police officer. The idea that farming was just as much of a dangerous profession as being a police officer seemed to be staring her in the face.

Zeke was a farmer.

She didn't want to lose another husband. She wanted to be safe.

She looked outside at the storm which seemed to be getting worse, with dark clouds rolling in, and the wind picking up even worse than it had been. It was one thing to have one night of danger, and the weather wasn't something that she could do anything about. Everyone was in danger tonight.

But to choose a profession, like farming, where an accident could happen any day, where a person worked with heavy equipment and never knew when something could go wrong, just like being a police officer.

"I was thinking we could make those iced sugar cookies that we made one year for Christmas. They were really popular, and people told us that we should make them and sell them. We don't have to make them in Christmas shapes, we can do any shape, and..."

Her mother droned on, and Annie tried to pay attention, but she looked at her watch. It had been exactly two hours since Zeke had left.

She looked down the road. He wasn't coming.

If he had some kind of problem, she couldn't help him. She didn't even have a vehicle.

Her heart started to beat hard, and her hands started to sweat. She could feel her breath coming in shallow gasps, and she felt the world spinning. A sense of gloom and doom fell over her, and she carefully took three steps to the couch so she could sink down.

"I need to go, Mom. Thanks for calling."

"Oh sure. Call me tomorrow and let me know how it goes."

"Of course," she said, hanging up and letting her phone drop to the couch.

She had to concentrate on breathing.

She was having a panic attack, and it was all because she allowed herself to think the scary thoughts.

She had to push them out of her head. She was going to be fine. People live through storms all the time. This house had weathered plenty of storms, and nothing was going to happen to Zeke.

Lord, I'm scared, and I know I shouldn't be. Please help me get a hold of myself and trust that You're going to work everything out.

Just the prayer alone reminded her that God was in control. He knew about the storm, and He could calm it if He wanted to. If He didn't, He would hold her hand while she walked forward.

Nothing was going to happen to them that was outside of His plan.

The idea calmed her, and her breathing evened out.

Still, she was frustrated with herself for allowing it to happen in the first place. She didn't have to always go to the very worst negative thing that could possibly happen, although it was probably mostly because her mom talked about the farmer who almost lost his life.

She wasn't going to think that just because something bad happened to someone else, something bad was going to happen to her too.

She thought she heard her children stirring upstairs and had turned to look up to see if the bedroom door had been opened, when her phone rang.

She grabbed it, thinking it might be Zeke.

Glancing at it, she confirmed that it was.

"Hello?" she said, hearing the anxiety in her voice and hating that she sounded scared.

"Hey, Annie. I hated to bother you, but I'm probably about a mile away. A tree has fallen down on the road, and I can't get through. I just wanted to let you know I was going to be a little longer because I'm going to have to walk the rest of the way."

"Oh. Are you okay?" The tree had fallen down on the road, not on his truck, right?

"I'm fine. But the wind is pretty bad and is definitely pulling branches and that type of thing down, although this is the first actual tree I've seen."

"I saw a four-wheeler in the shed. I can get the kids up and come get you."

"I'd prefer you don't. I think that when you have a situation like this, most of the time people who die in storms like these are people who are out in them. I am grateful that whenever the tree fell, it wasn't when I was going under it. I wouldn't want you to be coming to get me and have something like that happen."

"Oh. Okay." She didn't want anything to happen to her children, although she didn't want anything to happen to Zeke either, and the sooner he got back, the better.

She was tempted to get the four-wheeler and go get him anyway, but she didn't want to leave her children.

Just then, a thunderous roar made her whip around, just in time to see the huge old oak that had been in the yard with the tire swing on it fall, slowly at first, then with greater velocity until it hit the ground.

Branches covered the yard, but the tree didn't quite reach to the house.

"What was that?" Zeke asked.

"Oh my goodness. The oak tree, the one with the tire swing on it, it just fell."

"Are you okay?" Zeke asked, and it sounded like he was running.

"I'm fine. I'm fine. The house is fine." She looked out again. She could see the whole tree. But just then, rain started pouring down, mixed with small white balls that could only be hail. "Oh my goodness. It might have been safer for you to stay in your truck. It's raining and hailing here."

"Yeah. I can hear it, but it hasn't quite gotten here yet."

"Go back to your truck, please." She knew she was pleading, begging, but she wanted him to be safe.

"I'm halfway there now. It'll just be a few minutes."

She wasn't sure whether to believe that or not. But she didn't argue. She didn't want him to go back if it was truly going to take longer.

"I'd be there by now, but I wanted to bring the gas with me, because I still wanted to get some wood for the fire. Are you guys cold?"

She had been so scared she hadn't had a chance to be cold. But now that she thought about it, the air in the house was chilly.

"No. The kids are still sleeping, and I hadn't noticed until just now that it felt chilly in the house."

"I guess we have some wood that we can burn from the tree in the yard." He chuckled.

"Are you laughing?" she asked, listening to his chuckle, along with a deep breath with every step.

"Well, God provided wood for us, didn't He?"

And He kept them safe. So far. Although Zeke wasn't back yet. She supposed she wouldn't be satisfied that everything was going to be okay until he made it back.

"He did," she said weakly, sitting back down on the couch and trying to breathe deeply.

"Mommy?"

She wasn't sure whether she could be a mommy right now. She wanted someone else to be the mom, and she could curl up in their lap.

But no one else showed up, and so she said calmly, "It sounds like Justin's up. That means Braden's probably not far behind him. And I don't have any supper ready."

"The lights might go out. I'm not expecting them to, but I guess you never know."

She hadn't even considered that, and looking at her watch, she could see it was long past time for her to have started getting something ready.

"I'll let you go and see you in a few."

"Please be careful."

"Got it. I'll dodge any falling trees. Don't worry, I'll get there."

She shook her head and hung up, praying that he was closer than he realized and would be there in the next few minutes.

"I'm down here, sweetheart," she said when Justin called her name again.

Sometimes when they woke up from their naps, they were a little disoriented. Which was only natural. Sometimes she woke up disoriented.

"Can we go back to the creek?" Justin asked as he came down the stairs, sucking his thumb and holding his blanket.

"Not right now. You can look outside and tell me if anything looks different than it did before you went to bed."

She met Justin at the bottom of the stairs and gave him a hug, but he wiggled out of her arms and ran over to the window.

She moved to the kitchen, wondering what she could make that wouldn't take too long.

"Wow! Look at that!" Justin sounded so amazed, she had to smile.

"What? What happened?" Braden called from the top of the stairs.

"The tree fell down! It's all over the yard. It almost hit the house! This is so cool!" Justin sounded like it hadn't even occurred to him that someone could have gotten hurt from the tree falling down or that it might have hit the house.

Braden came storming downstairs and ripped over to the window to stand beside his brother. "Whoa! That's awesome," he said, and although Annie was still afraid, just seeing her boys be so excited made her smile.

She thought about how the Bible said to have a childlike faith. Their faith was so strong that nothing was going to happen to them that it didn't even occur to them to be afraid. She wished she had a faith like that. A faith that God was good, and that all the bad things she thought could happen wouldn't. That she could just be amazed at the size of the tree and how it fell and not upset about all the things that might have happened.

She pulled some hamburger out of the refrigerator and went into the pantry and got some pasta. It wouldn't be hard to make a pizza casserole with pasta and hamburger.

All the time she was working in the kitchen, she listened to her boys be amazed at the tree, at the wind, and at the things they were seeing, never thinking about their safety. All the while, she was saying a silent prayer for Zeke, that he would make it okay, that no trees would fall on him or anything else, and that he would be safe.

It wasn't just because she didn't want to spend the night here alone, but because the idea of something happening to him didn't just scare her, it hurt. Hurt in the way that a person hurt when someone that they cared about was in danger.

Still, to get her mind off all the things that could happen, she started humming a hymn.

One about trials and getting through them, and holding onto Jesus's hand and keeping her eyes on heaven.

She was just mixing the mozzarella cheese in with the pepperoni, hamburger, and pasta when Justin shouted, "Someone's walking up the driveway!"

She had forgotten to tell them that Zeke would be walking, not driving, when he arrived.

"We have to tell them that the tree is down!"

That made Annie laugh outright. Like he wasn't going to be able to see it.

"That's Zeke. There was a tree across the road, and he had to walk the last mile to the house."

"Can we go out and see him?" Justin said, his voice several notches louder than normal in his excitement.

"No. You guys just stay there. We don't know if any other trees are going to fall down, and I would prefer not to have you guys outside if they do."

The boys weren't very happy with her answer, but they went and stood by the door, waiting for him to come in.

"Mr. Zeke!" Justin said when Zeke opened the door and hadn't even set foot inside yet. "The tree!" He pointed at the tree that was in the yard, like Zeke hadn't had to walk around in order to get to the door. "It was like that when I got up from my nap! The wind must have blown it all down! Did you see it?"

Kids ask the silliest questions. It made Annie smile, even as she wiped her hands on a towel and hurried around the island.

The gas can sat outside on the step, and she supposed he was probably a little bit dirty, but she didn't care. She didn't stop until she had wrapped her arms around him and pressed close.

"I'm going to get you all wet. I'm soaked."

She hadn't even realized that the rain was still pouring down outside. There was so much gusting wind that at times it felt like the rain had stopped.

"I don't care. I'm so happy to see you. So happy that you're okay." She pulled back, her hands holding either one of his arms. "You are okay, right?"

"I am. Unless, I suppose if I say that I'm hurt somewhere, you'll give me even more attention?"

"Oh my goodness. You're not allowed to tease me at a time like this. You have no idea how worried I was."

He stepped in, shutting the door behind him, keeping an arm around her, pulling her to his side.

She put an arm around his waist and appreciated the human contact. She wouldn't mind holding onto him for the rest of the night and probably most of the day tomorrow.

"When it stops raining, I want to go out and cut some wood. It's cold in here."

"We can have a fire?" Justin asked, and Braden said, "Fire? Can I make a fire?"

"If we have a fire, neither one of you boys are going to be able to touch it. Fire is a very dangerous thing," Annie said, trying to infuse caution and authority into her tone.

Both of her boys' faces fell, but they understood from her tone that she meant business.

"Maybe, if the storm blows through, your mama will let you come out and help me haul firewood."

"I will. But I think everyone's probably hungry. And it's almost ready."

"Sounds good. I hope you don't mind if I run into my room and change my clothes. I'm soaking wet, and I don't want to get their house wet and dirty."

"Of course. Go change. I'm sorry, I didn't mean to hold you up."

"I didn't mind, I just feel bad that you're probably wet now too."

"I am, but I can change my clothes. And so far, we haven't lost electricity, so we can definitely do some laundry if we need to."

"I think the worst of the storm has passed, but we can check the weather when we get our clothes changed."

"You mean it's over?" Justin asked, sounding extremely disappointed. So heartbroken that it made Annie smile.

She met Zeke's eyes, and she read the same thing in his that she was feeling. That it was crazy the way the kids got so excited over a storm and never thought of the dangers.

Maybe some of that was foolishness, versus getting older and gaining wisdom, but so much of it was just total trust that God would work things out. They didn't even have to articulate it, because it was so ingrained in them to believe.

Zeke toed his boots off, and Annie tried to pull away to give him room. But he held on to her. And it didn't take much convincing for her to stay beside him.

Maybe they would talk about whatever was going on between them too. Although, he was a farmer. And the idea that there was a woman somewhere around Sweet Water who was sitting at the bedside of her husband this evening, unsure whether or not he was going to make it. Not knowing what their future held, and whether she would be facing it alone.

That weighed heavy on her mind.

Still, she wasn't going to think about that tonight but would remember to say a small prayer of thankfulness that God had brought Zeke home safely.

Chapter 22

Zeke poked the fire, glad that he had been able to go out and cut some wood to take the chill off the air in the house.

Tomorrow they would work on getting the tree in the yard cut up, and getting more dry wood cut they could burn in the house.

They could burn the wood from the tree that had just fallen down if they didn't have anything else, but dry wood would burn better with less smoke.

He had spoken with the homeowners and they'd said they would get a tree service to clean up the yard, but they were fine if Zeke had wanted to do it.

Zeke figured it would give them all something to do. The boys would enjoy helping, and he enjoyed working with Annie.

Thinking about her warmed his heart, but also gave it a bit of a squeeze.

He'd been worried about her being home by herself, and frustrated that he hadn't been able to get back to her as fast as he wanted.

He knew she was nervous anyway, and the delay had to have been hard on her.

She had and acted like it hadn't, had smiled and seemed like she was fine, but when he had put his arm around her, she leaned into him, and while most of him wanted to believe that it was because she was happy to see him, and that she liked him, there was a part of him that said it was more out of relief and fear.

A door clicked upstairs, and then Annie appeared at the top of them, slowly walking down, holding a brush in one hand.

He'd forgotten about her arm hurting, and stood from where he was kneeling in front of the fire, leaning the poker against the wall and walking over to the bottom of the stairs, meeting her as she reached the bottom.

"How's your arm?" he asked. "I'm sorry I forgot about it."

"It's fine as long as I don't reach up. I normally brush my hair with my right hand. I hope you don't mind, but I brought my brush down because I figured it would take a while since I'm going to have to do everything with my left."

"I can do it." He wasn't sure where those words came from. He hadn't really meant to say them. But he found he wanted to, and he held his breath while she looked up at him, searching his eyes as though trying to figure out why he would have said them.

He couldn't tell her, because he didn't know.

"Do you want to?" she finally asked, her face scrunching up like she couldn't believe it.

"My sister broke her arm once when we were little. I not only brushed her hair, but I put her makeup on, too. You might find I'm actually quite good at it."

He'd forgotten about that until just now. It seemed like such a long time ago, and he was just a kid. But, it was true.

Her eyes opened, and her brows lifted. "Really? You put her makeup on?"

He nodded. "She compelled me to do it. I agreed under duress. But I did get good at it. Truly."

She chuckled a little, and he was gratified to see her smile, to know he had caused it. It had seemed to become one of his goals in life, to see her smile.

He held his hand out, and she gave him an intent look for another two seconds before she gently put the brush in the palm of his hand.

"You can sit on the couch and I'll stand behind you," he said.

"I could sit on the floor and you could sit on the couch." She didn't bother to turn around to look at him before she went over and sat down directly in front of the fire, with her back to the couch.

He smiled and shook his head. That was like Annie, to give him the more comfortable spot, and not even make a big deal about it.

"I've noticed that you're willing to sacrifice pretty much anything for the comfort of your children. It seems... Maybe I'm included in that at times."

"You went the whole way down the mountain and back up to get us gas. You sacrificed your comfort for hours. Shouldn't there be a reciprocation of some sort?"

"Relationships don't have to have equal reciprocation," he said. Maybe that was the problem with a lot of relationships. A person did something nice and they expected that nice thing to be reciprocated immediately.

Sometimes there had to be periods of give-and-take, where a person was doing more giving than taking, and that had to be okay. After all, life wasn't fair, relationships were never equal, and someone was always getting or giving more than what they deserved or should.

"I agree. But, there should be reciprocation. Or it's not really a relationship, right?"

She stretched her legs out in front of her, her stocking feet pointing toward the fire which crackled cheerfully.

"That's right. I guess once you're in a relationship, a marriage, it shouldn't matter if the person that you're married to doesn't give back. But, ideally they should."

"That's not a popular opinion," she said casually as he stepped around behind her, so one leg was on one side of her shoulders and one leg was on the other before he sat down.

She leaned forward just a little to give him room to step in.

Her braid was long, reaching almost to her waist. Up until then, she'd always had it up, either in a braid or ponytail, and he'd never actually seen it completely down.

He found himself watching with fascination as her fingers deftly undid the braid, and she shook her hair loose around her shoulders and down her back.

He couldn't understand why his mouth was dry.

He cleared his throat. "It's not a popular opinion, but it's based on the Bible, so I would say it's the right one."

"I would agree with that," she said firmly, leaning forward a little as he pulled the brush through her hair.

It was soft, and slid easily over the calluses on his hands, hands that were a little sore from the wood he'd cut earlier. It was work he'd done plenty of times before, but wasn't exactly used to, and his hands ached a little.

Funny how the slide of her hair over them made them feel better.

They didn't say anything for a little bit, and he was tempted to close his eyes, just feel the softness of her hair, smell the scent of berries and vanilla which mixed with the wood smoke in the room, and gave such a down-home, comforting scent it almost brought tears to his eyes.

"I talked to my mom today," Annie said after a few minutes of silence as the fire crackled and he slowly brushed her hair.

Her words sounded soft, and maybe a little dreamy like him brushing her hair relaxed her.

He hoped it did.

"She okay?" he asked, unsure why she would have brought the subject up.

"She said that there was a farmer outside of Rockerton who had gotten caught in a piece of farm equipment and was in the ER. There's going to be a fund drive for him."

"That's too bad. But that's the hazard of farming I guess." He didn't understand why she was bringing that up, unless...maybe she wanted him to man the dunking booth again.

He was a little disappointed. He didn't really want to talk about fundraisers and dunking booths right now. Not with her hair in his hands and her scent in his nose and the relief of everyone surviving the storm safely.

He could hardly change the subject and tell her he thought he might be falling for her. So he kept his mouth closed.

"Yeah. It seems to me that farming is probably just as dangerous as being a police officer."

It took a minute for that to process. Then it shot off warning bells in his head and his hands froze, with the brush halfway down the strand of hair.

"I think everything's dangerous. Isn't it?"

"Some things are more dangerous than others, aren't they?" She shifted, turning to look at him, moving out from between his legs, her hair falling out of his hands. His hands dropped and his forearms rested on his knees, the brush held loosely in his fingers.

She was telling him something. Telling him that as much as he enjoyed brushing her hair, and loved being with her, she didn't want to go through what she'd already been through again.

It was pretty easy for him to see that.

His chest hurt. That wasn't what he wanted. He wanted more. He wanted everything.

But...

"Is there a chance that you would move off the Sweet Briar Ranch and do something other than farming for a living?" she asked, and her chin came up a little, the expression on her face belying the tremor in her words that showed how much she cared about his answer.

He wanted to say yes. That was not the honest answer. But he didn't want to lose her. Didn't want to lose the chance he had of being with the woman who felt perfect for him.

"Is there a chance that you would want to become a farmer?" he asked, knowing what her answer would be even as the words were coming out of his mouth. But he didn't know what else to say. He didn't want to leave Sweet Briar.

She shook her head. "It's too dangerous. My kids are not safe on the farm. I don't want them to be on the farm. And it's not because it's too much work, it's because... There's a man in the ICU right now, fighting for his life. His wife is sitting in the hospital crying. I've been there. I know how that feels." She took a breath, a shaky one, her chest heaving. "I don't want to do that again."

"And I don't blame you. I wouldn't want to do that again either."

He hesitated, knowing this wasn't the time for a lecture, but knowing that her reasoning was flawed.

"Isn't it more important to know for a fact that you're in God's will for your life, than it is for you to be "safe"?" he asked.

She pulled her lips in, biting them.

He set the brush to the side, and slid down to his knees on the floor, one hand on her leg, the other hand sliding his fingers and entwining them with hers.

"Tell me that you don't know that God is in control? That he has complete control over the farmer in the ICU, Merle, anyone. And everyone. God has it all under control. Each action is carefully orchestrated, and our responses to those actions show whether or not we trust him, believe that He is sovereign and good, or think that we somehow can do a better job than God."

He didn't mean to give her a hard time, didn't mean to imply that she wasn't trusting, or that she needed to be a better Christian. That wasn't what he was saying at all.

She took another breath, and then looked down at their joined hands. Her fingers limp, his radiating tension.

"I know you're right. But I feel like God has given me more than enough. With Merle...where was He?"

"Right here. He's always been right here." He said that with confidence. There was no doubt in his mind that God was right beside her all the way.

"Then why did Merle die? What good was there in that? How does that show any good for anything?" she asked, her words holding an edge of bitterness and anger.

"You wouldn't be here if it weren't for that," he said humbly. He hoped he wasn't being proud, and he hoped he wasn't overstepping. He held up their joined hands. "I'm not happy that Merle died. Don't think that at all. But this," he squeezed her hand. "This wouldn't be happening if Merle were still here. Maybe, maybe it doesn't mean anything to you, but I have the most amazing woman that I've ever met in my entire life sitting in front of me right now, holding my hand. She just let me brush her hair. Maybe that isn't special to you, and maybe it's not good, but if you hadn't suffered what you did, I wouldn't be sitting here tonight, hoping and praying that there is a chance for us to be more than casual friends."

Maybe it was the fire, maybe the storm. He wasn't sure exactly what it was that made him say things that he hadn't planned on saying at all. He didn't want to get ahead of her. To declare his feelings when she felt nothing.

But, he supposed it was what he was saying to her. A person couldn't have reward without risk. Pleasure without pain. Goodness without knowing what evil was.

He couldn't expect to move forward in a relationship with Annie if he wasn't willing to risk his heart. And yeah, risk the idea that she might not feel the same and he would feel pain.

He didn't want to be a coward, too scared to take a chance of letting her know how he felt, afraid that she wouldn't feel the same and he would be embarrassed. Good things didn't come to people who were afraid. They came to people who struck out in faith.

Willing to be knocked down, because they knew they could get up again.

Still, it felt like there was an awful lot riding on the silence as he searched her eyes, trying to find a clue of what she felt.

To his dismay, her eyes filled with tears. She pulled their clasped hands closer and bent until her lips touched his knuckle.

He wanted to move closer, to wrap his arms around her, because he hated the idea that she was crying, but he told her, at least gave a very large hint, about how he felt. Now he needed to wait.

"I'm scared," she said softly, her eyes downcast, her lips brushing his knuckle. "That hurt. It hurt a lot. I don't want to go through that again." She lifted her head. "You think God would make me go through that again?"

She shook her head quickly, as though she didn't want him to answer, and spoke right away. "If you weren't farming, there would be less of a chance. Surely it's not wrong for me to want you to be safe?"

It sounded like she cared. Like she didn't want him to be hurt. Like the idea of anything happening to him scared her like it would be Merle all over again.

"It's safer for me to be wherever God wants me, even if it's in the most dangerous position imaginable, because God's will is exactly where I'm supposed to be. Anything *else* is dangerous."

"Is it God's will for you to be a farmer?"

"A rancher. I was a Flyboy. Airplanes are dangerous. But, I could be living in the middle of the woods, in a big mansion with all the money in the world, and a tree could fall down on my house." He used his free hand to indicate the yard where the big oak tree lay. "There are plenty of trees that could have fallen down on this house and killed everyone. The tree that fell on the road could have fallen on my truck instead of in front of it. Lightning could have struck us, anything could have happened. It's a matter of trusting God for safety, and not being scared to do what we know He wants us to do."

He wanted to convince her that being with him was the smartest thing for her to do. But, he didn't want her to do something that she would regret. It had to be about her following the Lord, not about her following him.

"You're better off doing whatever God wants you to do, even if that leads you to a farm in North Dakota, than doing what you think you want to do." He looked at the fire, the cheerful flames at odds with the war in his heart. He wanted to say the pretty words, wanted to talk her into being with him. But, that wasn't the right thing to do. "With Merle dying, with all the things you had to handle after that, can you tell me honestly that you are the same person that you used to be? That you're not better? That God didn't use that to grow you and draw you closer to him?"

A little breath puffed out of her nose, almost as though she were giving a derisive snort. "I think maybe I chose to turn my back on God for a while. I chose to be more like a petulant child than an adult who had to grow and put one step in front of another. After all, I felt more bitter against God than anything."

"Do you think God made a mistake?"

Chapter 23

Annie sat in front of Zeke, her head down.

She'd loved him brushing her hair. She couldn't remember the last time someone had done that, and not only did it feel good and relaxing and comforting, but there was an element of attraction that it sparked that she couldn't, and maybe didn't want to, deny.

That his hands, so capable and strong, could be so gentle, was an entirely different idea, and she hadn't wanted it to end.

Hadn't wanted to think about the danger of his job and of being alone again. Of God taking everything that He'd given her, and leaving her alone.

Of her children growing up to be just like him, living that same dangerous life.

But she couldn't deny that he was right. That all of it had been orchestrated by the Lord. After all, she'd often thought about what huge odds there were against Merle being the one whose life was taken. Why him?

She hadn't considered that it had been something that God had done on purpose, to lead her through the valley, so she could emerge stronger and closer to Him, and that He had something even better He wanted to give her.

Zeke's question - did she think God made a mistake - hit the nail on the head. It encompassed everything she had been thinking. Because, if she didn't think Merle should have died, if she didn't think she should have been alone, if she didn't think that her husband should have been taken from her, then she had to admit that God was wrong.

And of course He wasn't.

"No. You're right. God didn't make a mistake."

"And whether you are a farmer, whether you're married to a farmer, whether I farm, whether I do something else, it doesn't matter. The Bible says safety is of the Lord. Whatever we do, God's hand of protection is over us, until it's not. And if it's not, it's because He is carefully orchestrating everything for our good, but most of all, for His glory."

She knew that. Maybe it was just something that she'd forgotten, because her life had been so upended when her husband died.

"Sometimes it's hard to remember God is good. Especially when bad things are happening."

"He sent his son to die for you. Do you really think that after all of that sacrifice, that pain, that suffering, that He's just going to turn his back on you and say forget it? Of course not. Because of all that pain-and-suffering he did for you, you can know that anything He works in your life is for your good."

"Maybe it's also because he wants to give me something better."

He had said something to that effect earlier, and she realized it was true. Merle was a good man, she wasn't trying to say he wasn't, but Zeke was a good man too. And here he was, just a few minutes ago telling her that he had feelings for her, but then, rather than shifting the course of his life to suit her, he challenged her to look at the Lord, and draw closer to Him.

That was the kind of man she needed. The kind of man God would want her to have.

But she also needed to know for sure that he wanted her.

"You want to be more than friends?" She lifted her eyes, a little scared, but knowing she needed to see his face as she spoke.

"I do. I... You know the reason that I went to the funeral and saw you afterward was because of Merle, but I couldn't get you out of my mind. I suppose that seeing you in Sweet Water was a shock. To say the least. But, it made me feel like maybe there was a reason I couldn't stop thinking about you. That God kept having our paths cross and here we are tonight, this week, together. I know that maybe there was some angling going on to get us here by the ladies in town, but there were a lot of things that had to fall in place in order for it to happen, although maybe that's secondary. After all, I've been feeling for a while that I want there to be more. Maybe you haven't?"

"I like the way you are with my kids."

Her heart beat fast. Her breath felt shallow. She was scared but she didn't want to not tell him how she felt. "And I like the way you are with me. I like the way you make me laugh. I like the way when you walk into a room you look for me, and your eyes stop moving when you find me."

"You noticed that?" he asked with a little smile. "I didn't even realize I was doing it. But you're right, I do."

"It makes me feel like you want to know where I am. That... You care. That I'm special to you." She took her other hand, and gently brushed it over the fingers she held. "I like your strength of character. I like just now that instead of pointing me to you, you pointed me to God, but in a way that you made clear that not only did you want the best for me, but you wanted me. If that makes sense."

"That's exactly right. That's exactly what I was trying to do. God is the most important, and what He wants is what we should do. But there's no doubt what I feel for you is not what I feel for my friends. It's more. A lot more."

She swallowed hard, and then said, "Same for me."

He smiled, a little bit of relief, a little bit of triumph, and she couldn't fault him for either emotion.

"If it came right down to it, if you want me to not be a farmer, I would leave Sweet Briar Ranch."

His other hand came up, and he threaded his fingers through her second hand, so that their hands were joined, and they were facing each other on the floor.

"But I don't think that's what God wants for us. I don't think God wants us to play it safe. I don't think He wants us to be scared, and make our decisions based on fear. I don't think He wants us to use the world's yardstick to measure what we should do with our lives. I think He wants us to look at Him. He wants us to follow Him. He wants us to understand that sometimes it's going to be a costly thing, to follow Him. That to lose our lives is to gain it. That to live boldly, to live in such a way that God gets the glory, not because we make ourselves comfortable, not because we give ourselves every little thing we want, but because we put God first, and we look around, seeing what we can do to be a blessing to others. Not saying we live foolishly. Taking unnecessary risks. I don't think that's what God wants. But He wants us to live day by day, making choices that build our character, that bless others, that show a total trust and dependence on God, and not on our intellect, whatever size it may be, and not on what the world calls common sense, or even intelligence. After all, Moses didn't act according to what the world around him considered to be intelligence. Neither did Abraham. Neither did Daniel. And Jesus certainly didn't either. God doesn't want us to play it safe."

It was a scary speech, and as Annie looked into Zeke's eyes, she wasn't sure whether to run in fear, or to throw her arms around him and hold on tight, hoping that some of his boldness, some of his confidence, some of his absolute trust in God would rub off on her.

But, one thing she felt for sure, she wouldn't be making a mistake to tie her life to someone who was so determined to do whatever it was that God wanted him to do.

"I wish I could be that... Sure of God."

He lifted one of their hands, and kissed her palm.

"I don't mean to give an impression that isn't true. I'm not saying I'm not afraid. Not saying I'm never doubting. I'm not saying that I never think that God is a little bit crazy, and maybe I'll reconsider the things He wants me to do. Not saying that at all. I'm just saying, as humans, as Americans, as people, we have a tendency to think that playing it safe is what Christians are supposed to do, but there's no place in the Bible that says that. None. And there's really no people in the Bible who lived life that way. It's not about being safe. It's about knowing life is going to require sacrifices. That following Jesus is not a safe life, not an easy life, but is the smart choice, and it's the best way."

"I know."

"Head knowledge sometimes doesn't always translate to action. And that's true for me. Just to be clear."

She nodded. Sometimes a person had to step out into fear. Into the blackness, into the unknown, and just trust that as long as they were doing what they were sure God wanted them to do, everything would work out.

"The problem is, my idea of things working out for my good, isn't always God's idea."

"I know. That's the scary part."

"Exactly."

"That's what requires faith. Childlike trust. Like your kids, not being afraid of the storm, meeting me at the door, excited to see me, they weren't scared or worried, that's the kind of attitude God wants us to have with our life. An attitude of excitement to see what's going to happen, not fear."

That was true, and she knew it, she just... "I don't know if I can do that."

"That's honesty."

"But I will try." She lifted her eyes to him. "Is it okay if I think that I might not be able to do it on my own, but I can do it beside you?"

He grinned a little, and brushed his lips over the palm of her hand again. The touch sent little sparks down her wrist to her elbow.

"Maybe that's why God gave us someone to walk through life with. Because He knew that we could lean on each other. The Bible even says that two are better than one. And God wouldn't have instituted marriage if He hadn't meant for a man and woman to pair up, because it's easier to face life when you have someone beside you."

"That's a comforting thought. And so true. Maybe that was part of the reason why it was so hard when Merle died. Facing life alone is scary and hard."

"But you're never truly alone."

"No."

"Then maybe it's harder to look at life by yourself, after you've been with someone. Because, I've been alone all this time, and I have to admit, it hasn't been a scary or difficult thing, but the idea that I might get to walk beside you for the rest of my life has me excited, and I don't want to think about how it's going to hurt if you turn me down."

She squinted. Pursing her lips, and smiling just a little.

"That was not a marriage proposal."

He laughed, and maybe a little of the spell was broken. Or maybe the laughter just served to tighten the feeling of the two of them belonging together.

"It was a pretty bad one, if it was, wasn't it?"

"I don't know. It was unique, anyway."

"I don't want to push you too fast. Marriage is forever."

"Until death parts us." She knew that from experience.

He lifted his chin, and then nodded. "That's right. You should know."

"I do. But, talking to you tonight has helped me look back on what happened in a new light. Looking at it like God knew what was best all along, and I just didn't have the full picture. I still don't. I still maybe won't know all the things that happen because of Merle dying. I do know you're right about tonight. And, I really wouldn't want to miss tonight. So far it's been pretty amazing."

"So far?"

She leaned forward, pulling her hands from his, and placing them on his shoulders, before she moved her arms around him, pulling close until just a couple of inches separated them.

"So far. I suppose there are a few things that could make it better."

"I'm listening."

"You could make that marriage proposal a little more clear. You could wait until I said yes. And then you could kiss me. I'm pretty sure that would be a perfect night."

His smile was slow, his lips curving out as her heart beat harder. Although she wasn't sure why she was nervous. Obviously her words had been exactly what he wanted to hear.

His arm slid around her back, and his head bent closer, his lips brushing her temple.

""Would you be interested in marrying me?" he asked, and his voice next to her ear, sending shivers down her spine, and making her hands clench on his back.

"Yes."

It was crazy. The idea that she could be so sure about something. So eager to commit to something that would bind her for the rest of her life. But, Zeke had shown her this evening where his loyalty lay, and she didn't think there was anything she could do that would be smarter than to choose her life partner to be someone who was following God so closely.

"I can't believe you said yes," he said.

"You just told me I needed to live boldly. To not be afraid. To do what I know God wants me to do. There was no other answer."

His lips skimmed down her cheek and touched the corner of her mouth.

"I think there was one more thing you said I needed to do in order to make this a perfect night."

"And if you don't get moving on it, I'm going to do it for you."

That made his lips turn up again, but he didn't wait to see if she would do what she said she was going to do. His mouth covered hers, and as his arms tightened, and her heart beat harder, and her world tilted and shifted, she clung to him, feeling like he was the only steady thing, while her chest felt like it could burst for happiness.

Maybe there was some truth, a lot of truth, in the fact that in order for her to feel like this, she had to go through the suffering first. That made tonight, and the outlook of the rest of her life, so much sweeter, because she knew how it felt to not have it. She knew how precious it was. Knew what it was like to be alone and appreciated the blessing of having a man who cherished her, who wouldn't bend his principles, or stop following the Lord, because of her fear, or her disbelief.

Chapter 24

"Good job, Chewy," Ellen said, as they finished their practice run, and she stood watching the other competitors with their cattle dogs.

This was their first big competition, and Ellen had to admit she was nervous.

She'd written to Travis, letting him know that she would be competing, and that she wasn't sure how it was going to go.

She stopped short of asking him to be there with her.

She wasn't sure if that was breaking the boundaries of their friendship or not. She tried to respect the boundaries he set. After all, she didn't want to be a stumbling block to him. She wanted him to reach his full potential, and to do everything God wanted him to do. If that meant he was doing it without her, then she supposed that was the way it needed to be.

Hopefully, sometime in the future, God would plan again for them to be together, but until that point, Ellen had to let go of what she wanted, and just allow things to be.

To do her very best, without having expectations about what her life should look like.

Although, she wouldn't mind taking home a trophy today. Her life could look like that.

"You guys are gonna do just fine," Ashley said, coming over and standing beside Ellen.

She'd gotten someone to watch the baby - he wasn't such a baby anymore - so Tadgh and she could support Ellen in her first competition.

"Do you think?" Ellen said, even though she knew she was supposed to just agree with Ashley.

"I've seen you work. I've seen how she responds to you. You have the best dog here. Now, maybe both of you are a little bit nervous because this is your first competition, but to win your first competition would be a huge accomplishment. If you just finish, if you do everything you're supposed to do, even if you don't do it perfectly, I think that's a win. Even if you don't end up with a trophy for it."

Her words made Ellen feel a little bit better. She didn't have quite as much pressure on herself. Even though she didn't enter competitions just to finish. She entered them to win.

She felt like Chewy understood. Usually she was a goofball, constantly moving, and trying to play with everything in her path. But, today, she stood with her ears pricked, whining deep in her throat, looking around at the strange sights and sounds.

It had been a year and a half that Ellen had been training her, which was a long time to spend training a dog, but since it was Ellen's first, she made a few mistakes that she had to untrain, and retrain the correct way.

"Tadgh said we'd go for ice cream afterwards if you wanted to," Ashley said, her hand on Ellen's shoulder.

Ellen leaned into her, she might be fifteen, but she still felt like a child at times. She was competing against adults in this competition, which made her feel even more so.

"I think, whether I win or lose, ice cream would be wonderful." And she meant that. If she didn't win, which was quite possible, she could drown her sorrows in creamy sweetness. And if she did win, it would be a nice reward. Something to look forward to anyway.

A man's voice over the loudspeaker started calling dogs to the starting line, and the first competitors lined up.

"I better go back and sit with my husband. But I just wanted you to know we're pulling for you, like you didn't already."

Of course they were. They spent three hours driving to this competition, and had given up the entire day for her. Ellen knew they loved her, and she knew they were behind her completely.

Looking around again, she wished Travis were there. It was futile, she was sure. But, she couldn't keep her heart from longing for him.

"We're friends. We're just friends," she whispered to herself as Ashley walked away and she was left alone with Chewy and God. Kneeling down, she put her arm around Chewy, who licked her cheek with her slobbering tongue, panting beside her.

It wasn't that hot, and Ellen figured she was just nervous, the same as she was.

She lifted her eyes to sweep over the stands and spectators one more time. But, there was no sign of the tall slender boy with dark eyes, staring at her.

So she shoved that thought aside, and tried to focus on doing her very best.

The competitors were a little distracting to Chewy, and she had a little bit of trouble when their turn came, getting Chewy to focus on the sheep, and not on the other dogs, or the people that milled around.

Still, Chewy's small lack of concentration, and the two commands that Ellen gave that she shouldn't have, weren't enough to keep them from taking the trophy home.

As they were walking toward their truck, Chewy following at her heels, Tadgh's arm around her shoulder, and Ashley carrying her trophy, Ellen thought she might possibly have seen a tall, dark-eyed boy staring at her from across the other side of the field.

She couldn't be sure, and she didn't want to make a big deal by stopping and looking.

She'd never confided to Ashley, and she certainly never told her uncle about her teenage crush.

They thought her world revolved around her Highland cattle and the training she did with Chewy. And, for the most part it did.

That, and helping her uncle and Miss Ashley with their business on the farm, and occasionally with Ashley's graphic design business, and with the baby when they needed her.

Stealing one more glance over her shoulder, she saw that whoever it was she'd seen, was gone.

That was probably just as well. The sooner she realized that Travis had been serious when he said that they were going to be friends, and he had meant distant friends, the better.

Chapter 25

It was a lovely morning for Zeke to spend outside cutting the tree with both boys. He had them sit on the porch if he was cutting anything that might fall, but once he had the logs on the ground, they came over and carried the little pieces that they could lift back to the woodpile.

They'd probably been working for thirty minutes or so before he saw Annie's head in the door window.

His whole chest expanded, and he had to fight to keep the silly grin off his face.

Last night felt more like a dream than reality, but he saw the soft look in her eyes and the sweet smile on her face, and he knew it was real.

He certainly hadn't begun the day thinking that he was going to ask her to marry him. He felt a little bad because he hadn't had a ring or plan or anything, but she hadn't seemed to mind. He said a lot about following God, and it seemed to resonate with her, which had said to him that she was perfect.

He didn't want a woman who was going to argue with him over whether or not he should follow the Lord. Over wanting him to do easy things just because it would make her comfortable.

Annie had clearly agreed with him, even though she didn't say that it was going to be easy, which he figured was a good thing. Anyone who expected life to be easy was bound to be disappointed.

He thought she might stay inside and start on lunch, but a few minutes later, she had her boots and jeans on and was walking toward them with gloves on.

He'd gotten way ahead of the boys, and after their eyes met and they exchanged smiles, she bent over and gathered up a load of firewood in her arms, talking to her boys as they walked around the house to the pile of wood.

He kind of had it in his head that he wanted to have the yard cleaned up as much as possible before they left in a few days. Not because anyone was expecting it of them, but just because it was their job to watch the house, and since it happened on their watch, and since he had the skills necessary to clean it up, he felt he should.

Plus, he liked working with Annie and her boys. Liked the idea that they would be a family soon and enjoyed spending time with her, no matter whether they were sitting in front of the fire with him brushing her hair or stacking firewood.

Well, he definitely had a preference over which one he would prefer to do, but he enjoyed her company either way.

They worked for another hour, with Braden losing interest and going to play over on the side of the yard with some sticks and sawdust.

He was impressed that Justin worked beside his mom, and figured that it had everything to do with the boy wanting to spend time with her and her setting a good example for him.

Another notch in Annie's favor, like she needed any more. He'd already known that she would go to great lengths to set a good example for her children, even when she didn't feel like it. That was just more proof.

They had about half of the tree cleaned up when he shut his chainsaw off, and watched Annie as Justin walked toward him.

When Braden heard the chainsaw shut off, he jumped up from where he was playing and ran over, grabbing his mom's hand, and dancing around her.

"Is it time to eat yet?" Braden asked with excitement.

Annie smiled with affection at her son, and said, "I probably should go in and get something started."

"Want me to help you?" he asked. "It seems like it's only fair if I give you a hand, since you've been out here helping me all morning."

"I'm not going to turn down help," she said easily.

Figuring he would come back and work some more after lunch, he set the chainsaw down where he'd been working, dusted his pant legs, and stepped over the log he'd been cutting.

"I have an idea for a meal. I'll just need to check and make sure we have all the ingredients."

"Really?" she said, sounding surprised.

"What? Are you surprised I'm offering to cook, or that I can?"

"Either? Both?"

He laughed, putting his arm around her, and setting his other hand on Justin's shoulder.

"You were a good help this morning, kiddo," he said to Justin, squeezing his shoulder just a bit, as they started toward the house.

"I helped too!" Braden said from the other side of Annie.

"Sure did. I appreciated both of you. And your mom, she did a good bit as well."

"Always kind of you to remember me," Annie said with a smile in her voice.

He wasn't sure he'd ever seen her this happy. Not bubbling and effusive, but just smiling and content.

It made him feel good that perhaps he had a little bit of something to do with that. Whether it was the idea of them being together, or whether it was something he had said about trusting the Lord, even when it was hard. Knowing that God was going to walk them through hard things.

He didn't care, he was just happy that she was happy, and that she seemed to have settled something in her mind that had given her a spirit of joy and peace.

It looked beautiful on her.

He wanted to lean over and tell her that she was beautiful, but it didn't seem like the right place or time.

But then, he figured it didn't really matter, did it? He didn't have to wait for the right place and the right time to say the truth.

"You're beautiful. There's a glow about you that makes you almost irresistible. I just want to be with you."

There. That was the truth.

"Maybe that's because I'm with you. That would make anyone happy, wouldn't it?"

"Hardly," he said, knowing that was true. It wasn't just any woman who would be happy with him. After all, look how badly he'd fumbled the marriage proposal last night. He rushed it, pushing too hard and too fast, but she understood what was in his heart, and looked at that, rather than his bumbling ineptitude at romance.

"I think so," she said as he opened the back door and they walked in.

"I think I'd better go change my clothes. I don't want to get sawdust all over the kitchen, then I'll look that recipe up on my phone."

"All right. I'll trust you to know what you're doing."

"I like it," he said, and then he did what he'd wanted to do since she walked outside.

He leaned down and kissed her.

"Ew. Mr. Zeke just kissed mommy. That's gross." Braden wriggled his nose. It wouldn't have surprised Zeke if he would have held it with his fingers. Like there was something stinky.

"That's okay. I like mommy, and I like Mr. Zeke too." Justin shrugged his shoulders like it wasn't a big deal, and finished taking off his boots.

Zeke caught Annie's sigh, and lifted his brows. She shrugged one shoulder, and lifted her lip.

He took that to mean that it was up to him whether he was going to say something or not. He figured he might as well.

"I hope you don't mind if I kiss your mom. I'm planning on marrying her."

"So you'd be our dad?" Justin asked, and he didn't seem upset about the idea. Although, he didn't seem extremely excited about it either.

"I'd like to be. Would that be okay?" He was going to add a bunch of stuff about not taking their real dad's place, but he wasn't sure whether, at three and four, Justin and Braden were ready for words like that.

Plus, he hadn't really talked to Annie about how they would handle it. And, he supposed that maybe as they grew they'd want to handle it differently. Regardless, if he were marrying Annie, he would be treating the boys like his own. That much he knew. He couldn't really dictate how they treated him.

"I guess. Does that mean I call you daddy?"

Zeke wasn't sure he was ready for that. He hadn't even thought about it, but thankfully he didn't have to answer because Annie stepped in.

"You can. Or you can call him Mr. Zeke, or even Dad. It's up to you. As long as you speak respectfully to him. The way you would any adult."

Justin shrugged his shoulders and said okay, then, he didn't say what he had decided to do, and instead, tore his shirt off, stepped out of his pants and went running up the stairs, with Braden not far behind him.

"I guess they're typical boys who can't wait to get out of their clothes." He watched them go with bemusement.

She laughed. "I guess I better go make sure they get cleaned up."

"All right. I'll be in the kitchen."

He almost let her go, then he touched her arm.

She turned, surprise on her features as she searched his face.

"Thanks."

He wasn't sure whether he was thanking her for the answer she gave to her son, or that she wasn't insisting that Merle's memory be sacred. He didn't want to step on Merle's shoes, but at the same time, Merle wasn't here anymore and he was.

Or maybe he was thanking her for helping him. For coming out and being beside him. For not being afraid to get dirty, and for allowing her children to help as well. For being with him, and spending time with him.

Or, maybe it was something else.

"You're welcome?" she said, as though she to had no idea what he was thanking her for.

It wasn't often that he said words and he wasn't even sure what they meant. It was even less often that he followed that up with silent action, rather than an explanation, but this time he did. Stepping forward, he put his arms around her and lowered his lips to hers.

She didn't hesitate, but wrapped her arms around him, pulling his head down, and kissing him back with an emotion that surprised him.

He supposed lunch could have been really late, but there was a bang upstairs, which caused them to break apart.

"I did... I better go see what that is," Annie said, sounding like she was still getting her bearings, but knew she had a responsibility as a mother.

"Yeah. Yell if you need me," he said, wishing he didn't need to step back and drop his arms, but doing it anyway.

Their gazes lingered, before she turned and hurried out of the mudroom, and a few seconds later her footsteps sounded on the stairs as she hurried up.

Figuring that he needed to think about food to get his mind off of Annie, he tried to recall a dish that he had made back in the Air Force with a couple of guys who had been stationed overseas. Vietnamese lemon chicken, he thought it was called.

Hurrying into the bedroom, he changed his clothes quickly, and grabbed his phone, looking up a recipe that looked somewhat similar to the one that he had made before.

Then, he strode to the kitchen, looking to see if it was as well-stocked as what he had thought it was.

The homeowner had been in the Air Force too, and maybe he'd picked up a taste for a few exotic dishes, because all of the ingredients were there.

He had most of them out on the counter by the time Annie came back.

The boys, fresh faced and clean, ran into the kitchen ahead of her.

It took a little while, but they worked as a family to get dinner on the table. While it was baking, they played some board games and found a pack of balloons that the boys enjoyed playing with.

By the time dinner was over and they had cleaned up, he washed the dishes while Annie put the kids down for a nap.

He was just finishing up, and wondering if he should go outside or wait on her, when his phone rang.

"Hello?" he said, putting it in one hand while he wiped the counter with the other.

"Zeke. How are things going with the housesitting?" Miss April asked, her voice recognizable anywhere.

"Going well. Had a little bit of a storm last night, and a tree fell in the yard, but we've been cutting it up and stacking it for firewood. What's up?"

"Well, a farmer from just south of Sweet Water, in Rockerton, was injured in a farm accident and is in the ICU in Rockerton. We're organizing a benefit for him, and —"

"Let me guess. You want me to man the dunking booth again."

Zeke interrupted her, knowing that he shouldn't have. It was rude for one, but he didn't want to hear about the farmer who was struggling. It was too close to what he and Annie had talked about last night. In fact, that was probably the farmer that had upset her.

He couldn't tell her that farming wasn't dangerous. And he couldn't say that people didn't have accidents every day.

A benefit probably wasn't something she was going to want to participate in, and he didn't want to give her a chance to change her mind.

But he also couldn't turn down Miss April. He couldn't turn down the opportunity to help.

"Oh no," Miss April said with a laugh. "I was hoping that you and Annie would spearhead the goat milking competition."

"I can't talk for Annie, but I guess I can do it. Although I've never done it before. Is there a specific way it has to be done?"

"You're in charge, you can do whatever you want to. But if you want to talk to a few people who have done it before, I can get you in touch with them, so you can have an idea of how they handled it."

"I'll take you up on that. Text me their numbers."

"All right. I'll do that. Do I need to call Annie or can you ask her?"

"She's upstairs putting the kids to bed, but I'll ask her when she comes down and send you a text and let you know what she says."

He didn't want to, didn't want to say he would ask, but thought that maybe it would be better coming out of his mouth than someone else's.

"All right. I expect to hear from you this afternoon sometime."

Miss April thanked him and then hung up.

Zeke swiped his phone with a sinking feeling in his stomach. If anything was going to cause Annie to come face-to-face with the fact that she could end up with a second husband who had gone the way the first, this was it.

But, Zeke figured that maybe it was a good thing. He supposed it would be bad for them to actually get married if Annie was going to back out at some point. Worse, or maybe just as bad, if she were going to try to talk him out of doing what he knew the Lord wanted him to do. He had no doubt that he was supposed to be in Sweet Water, that he was working on what God had for him in his life. After all, he'd met Annie here, and he knew that was something the Lord had ordained.

Realizing his thoughts were close to worry, he shoved them aside.

"That's a serious face," Annie said as she walked into the kitchen.

"Miss April called."

"What did she want?" Annie asked, the smile that she had as she walked in turning into a serious expression of worry.

"You know the man you told me about yesterday? The farmer who was in the hospital?"

"Is he okay?" Annie asked, her hand going to her chest.

"I guess; he's still alive anyway."

"That's good," Annie said, letting out a little breath.

"They're having a benefit for his expenses, and Miss April called wanting to know if you and I would do the goat milking competition."

"That's better than the water dunking booth," Annie said immediately.

"I told her I would text her and let her know what you said," Zeke said, unable to laugh with her. Figuring that she needed a few minutes to process and realize what they were doing.

"As long as I'm doing it with you, I'll do whatever they want. But, I have to warn you, I know nothing about milking goats."

"I don't know much about that either. I guess we'll learn together." Zeke shook out the rag, laid it flat on the table, and then turned to face Annie, leaning against the counter and crossing his arms over his chest.

"Are you sure you're okay with this?"

She tilted her head and narrowed her eyes a little as she stepped toward him.

"Why are you looking so serious?" she asked, as though she were trying to figure it out.

Surely she understood what this meant, and why it would scare him, but she acted like she didn't have a clue.

She stopped right in front of him, putting her hands on his forearms, and looking up into his eyes.

He couldn't keep his arms crossed with her right in front of him. He opened them, she stepped in and he closed his arms around her, holding her tight, feeling her warmth against him and loving that she hadn't run at the first opportunity.

"I thought it might remind you of your fear of accidents, and your idea that farming was dangerous."

"Farming is dangerous," she murmured. "But you said, and you're right, that it's more dangerous to be out of the Lord's will."

That was all she said, and it was a simple thing, but it was all he needed to know. She made up her mind, and she wasn't going back.

"I love you. I guess I should've told you that yesterday. If I weren't such a bumbling idiot, and so terrible at anything that has to do with romance, or making a woman feel special, I probably would've said it then."

"I love you too. And I don't really care how good you are at romance. If you want to get better, I know you will. It's not like you have to stay the way you are."

He leaned his head on top of her hair, breathing in her berries and vanilla scent and smiling. That was so right. After all, she had struggled through depression, to come out on the other side. To be happy, to push her fear away, and face the future with excitement and expectation. To trust God even though he had led her through some hard valleys.

"Do you know anyone who might be willing to give me a hand? Teach me what I need to know to make this woman that has bravely agreed to marry me feel special and loved?"

"We might be able to find someone who will give you some lessons, but I think you're doing pretty good on your own," Annie's words were spoken against his neck, then she pulled back a little looking up into his face. "Maybe you can help me."

"Help you?"

"Surely there are things I could do better."

"I can't think of any. Not a single one." And that was the truth. All he wanted was for her to be with him. To help him, to smile at him and make his world sweeter with her presence. There really wasn't anything else he could ask. Maybe someday he'd figure out the words to tell her that too.

Chapter 26

"Looks like Lily has more than Sherry, so Lily wins." Annie said as the girls held up their measuring cups full of milk.

Actually, Sherry's had less than a quarter of a cup of milk in it. She just hadn't been able to get the hang of the way her fingers needed to work in order to get milk out of the goat.

Some people picked it up right away, and some people struggled.

Regardless, everyone seemed to have fun. And the crowd definitely loved cheering them on.

Zeke handed Lily her prize, a coupon from the diner for a free meal for her and a guest.

The mood at this benefit was a little bit more somber than the spring festival, but people were still smiling and having fun.

The cloud of a man whose life was in the balance definitely shadowed things, but they had had some good news in the last few days, and it looked like he might be getting out of ICU soon.

Regardless, his medical bills were going to be astronomical, and everyone was pitching in as much as they could to make this benefit successful.

Her mom had her kids, which made it easier for her to work.

The goats were almost completely milked out, and they would be closing down their booth before long.

"You good?" Zeke said as he put an arm on her shoulder waiting for her to look up at him.

"I am."

She knew he was concerned about her changing her mind. But, the night that they had talked in front of the fire had solidified in her heart all the things she knew but hadn't been holding onto over the past year.

God loved her, and He wasn't going to take her through the valley of pain and sorrow without holding her hand through it all. Without bringing her through the other side stronger. Without giving her beauty for ashes.

"What's that look for?" Zeke said. He had started to turn away, but whatever was on her face had drawn him back.

"I just really appreciate you." And she appreciated that the Lord had given him to her.

"Zeke? Annie?"

Annie jerked her gaze from Zeke to turn toward the person who had just said their names.

She recognized the wife of the farmer in the hospital. Kristi Neel.

"Kristi. How's Dave?" Her heart broke for Kristi when her face fell.

But then, she forced her lips up into a smile, and took a breath. "He's about the same. But, I just wanted to come over and thank you for helping. Both of you. I really appreciate the whole town coming together the way they have to support us. It's... It's going to be hard."

"That's what we've heard. You know if there's anything we can do, we'll give you a hand however we can." Zeke put an arm around her shoulders, and they both took a step toward Kristi.

"I know that. That is so reassuring. That, and knowing that God is good is all that has gotten me through these last dark days." She took his hand and squeezed it.

"I know we'll get through this. Somehow. And, if there's ever anything that I can do in return, please just ask."

"You don't need to worry about returning anything. Just focus on taking care of your husband, and helping him get better."

"Thanks. I know you know the pain of loss, and that means a lot coming from you."

Annie smiled, and realized it made her feel good to know that Kristi was taking comfort in the fact that she had gone through something hard and made it through. Maybe that was what the Lord had in mind. Allowing her to be an example to other people, so they could look at her and be encouraged through their own trials.

She wasn't sure whether that was exactly what God had planned or not, but it seemed like it was at least a good benefit.

"All right. I'm sorry I need to run off, but I wanted to try to thank everyone and then I need to get back to the hospital. Dave was undergoing a procedure, and I had a few hours free. I knew this was going on, and I just wanted to thank people."

"I'm sure most people feel the way we do. That we'll do anything to help. Just let us know."

"Thank you."

Kristi turned and hurried away, and for a moment, Annie and Zeke watched her go.

"You encouraged her," Zeke said simply.

"I got that feeling too. Even though I really didn't do anything. In fact, I spent most of the last year in a depression, but..."

"But you're happy today. And it shows her that you can be sad, and have something awful happened to you, and that life goes on. That you smile and find happiness again."

"Maybe that is because of you."

"And the Lord."

Of course. God had given her a man just as good, maybe even better, then the one she lost. All she had to do was open her eyes and see that.

They helped the last few people to milk the goats, before Henry Bollinger, who owned them, came to take them home.

They gathered their children, and started walking down the street toward Annie's house.

The kids were chattering as they walked. Until they saw Billy standing on the sidewalk in front of their house, and the kids ran to pet him.

"I thought they had a petting zoo with him in it today?" Zeke said.

"I know they did, but maybe they finished a little early?" Annie said, wondering how Billy had gotten out of the petting zoo to their house since they seem to have left before most of the other people.

"You know, I don't want to push you or anything, but I was wondering if you were thinking about a date. Or maybe you want to hold off till you get used to the idea?"

"I don't need to hold off. I'm ready whenever you are."

"I just think it would be easier if we were together on the farm. I... Don't always go with what's easier, but...all right. Maybe I should just admit that the idea of going back home and being without you isn't one that I want to entertain. I'll miss you. And... I like to have you with me."

"Same," she said, looking up into his face and smiling.

"All right then? What were you thinking?"

"Today? Tomorrow?"

He laughed. "That's a little faster than what I was thinking, I'm totally down for it if that's what you want. I'm certainly not going to argue."

"Are you sure?" she asked, her eyes twinkling, because she was pretty sure he thought he was going to be the one pushing her to get married before she was ready, and she thought maybe she had ended up taking him by surprise.

"I'm sure. Do you want to drive into Rockerton this afternoon?"

"This afternoon sounds fine. Should we take the boys?"

As she suspected, his eyes widened at her easy agreement.

"Are you sure?"

"Are you trying to talk me out of it?"

"I just can't believe it."

"I can't think of anything else I'd rather do."

He looked at her for a moment, as though trying to judge whether her words were true or not, and she didn't allow herself to be offended. After all, it was kind of unbelievable, and certainly not the way normal people did things. But, she'd never been very good at being normal.

"All right. Let's load up the boys and take a trip this afternoon."

"Sounds good. Maybe we should kiss on it."

He laughed outright, but it didn't take long for him to lower his head and do exactly what she suggested.

Enjoy this preview of *Just a Cowboy's Dream Come True,* just for you!

Just a Cowboy's Dream Come True

Chapter 1

Carna Long put her car in park and stared at the farmhouse and grounds.

Sweet Briar Ranch.

A new start. A new life.

Beside her on the passenger seat, Posey whined and stretched, lifting her head and pointing her nose in the air as though better able to catch the scents that drifted in through the partially open window.

"Hang on a second, Posey," Carna murmured, needing a moment to compose herself.

Her brother, Smith, had told her there would be a job for Posey and her here and a place to stay.

Everything she owned was in the car she drove, which had miraculously held together on the long trip from New Hampshire.

She'd tried as hard as she could to save her grandparents' farm, but in the end, the only thing she'd saved had been Posey.

She hadn't quite gotten over that bitter disappointment and had a hard time mustering any enthusiasm to be in North Dakota, although she appreciated the fact that she had a job and family. Her brother. Even if she didn't know him that well since it had been years since they'd spent any amount of time together. Not only because of Smith's time in the Air Force, but because Carna had been busy working day and night trying to keep their grandparents' farm from going bankrupt.

Her eyes swept the area in front of her again. She'd texted Smith just a bit ago and let him know she was coming, but she didn't see him, or anyone, around. Then she blinked and did a double take.

There was a Highland steer standing beside the chicken coop.

She'd seen pictures of Highlands, and was vaguely familiar with them, but had never been close to one. Still, it was unmistakable with the shaggy fur and the long horns.

Horns that, unless she was mistaken, had just gotten caught in the latch of the chicken coop, and...as he shook his head, the latch jiggled open and the door swung wide.

The steer moseyed away, like he hadn't noticed that he had just opened the coop door, but the chickens had no such compunctions.

As a unit, they flew and ran for the door, like some sort of signal had gone through the entire fenced chicken yard, one that sent them all running for freedom.

Posey whined as Carna grabbed her door handle to get out.

"All right. You can come." Posey was used to working on the farm. Maybe it was Carna's imagination, but she seemed to get more depressed the further away they got from New Hampshire, like she knew she was never going to see her home again.

Knowing the chickens were soon going to be too scattered to even attempt to round up, Carna hopped out of the car, holding the door for Posey to jump out, then slammed it and jogged over to the melee.

But she was too late. It would be impossible to catch the chickens now. They would have to wait until evening when they roosted. Chickens were always easier to catch at night. They had a tendency to not move around much at all once darkness fell. Of course, finding them wherever they roosted would be the challenge.

Just then, barking made her jerk her head to the right as a dog, low to the ground, ears back, raced toward them, startling and chasing first one chicken and then another.

"Hey!" Carna said, going forward, even though she knew it was dangerous to attempt to grab a strange dog. But still, she couldn't just stand there while it attacked the chickens and possibly killed them.

"Pepper. Down!" a deep male voice called, and the dog stopped immediately, falling to the ground in a crouch, his ears back, his head rolling to the side as he looked for the man who had called to him.

The man, clad in jeans and a T-shirt with worn low-heeled, square-toed work boots and a cowboy hat pulled low over his eyes, walked toward her.

Because of the hat, she couldn't see the expression on his face other than his flat lips, which sliced a thin line over his square and jutting jaw.

A muscle twitched there.

He was angry, and Carna had to fight back the shot of anxiety that zipped through her. She hadn't done anything wrong. She tried to calm herself by saying that she didn't have to worry about his anger, because it was not going to be directed at her.

"Ma'am. You need to get back in your car and go to the guest entrance. This is our private quarters. And you don't ever open an animal pen without permission. Whether here or at anyone else's ranch." The man didn't exactly snarl at her, but it was obvious he was holding onto his patience by a fraying thread.

Carna opened her mouth and then closed it again. He thought she was a guest?

She wore jeans and boots and a T-shirt, similar to his outfit, although several sizes smaller most definitely, and she didn't have the cowboy hat. Back east, her boots were pushing the limits of what people thought was ridiculous; the cowboy hat would practically land her in queue for the insane asylum.

Still, she had to defend herself. The man was mistaken.

"I didn't open the chicken door. The steer did it."

The man stumbled, then caught himself immediately. He snorted and then lifted his hat, running a hand through his hair as though he needed a moment to compose himself so that he could speak lucidly.

"Of course. The steer opened the chicken pen." He shook his head. "Now I've heard it all. Lady, get back into your car, go back to where the road forks, and take the other lane. That will take you to the guest quarters. They can deal with you there."

"I sure hope you're not dealing with guests. As rude as you are," Carna mumbled, unable to keep her opinion to herself when she knew she should.

Still, the man was odious and arrogant. The idea that she would lie. Of course, the idea that the steer opened the chicken pen was probably just as laughable to him as it was to her.

"I'm not a guest," she managed to say to the man as he took two steps away from her, like their conversation was finished.

"Then you're a trespasser," the man said flatly. It wasn't a question.

"I belong here. I'm Smith's sister, Carna. And you are?" She held out her hand and tried to keep the superior note out of her voice. Smith might not be the sole owner of the place, but she knew for a fact that the Sweet Briar Ranch had been started by Smith's crew, and Smith was the commander. Regardless of whether they were out of the Air Force or not, he would be given an extra dose of respect, if she didn't miss her guess.

The man froze, then he turned toward her slowly, his eyes narrowed, his head slightly tilted as though he were trying to see something in her that he expected to be able to pick out.

The look made her uncomfortable, like she was hiding something.

Not to mention, she felt stupid with her hand out while the man made no move to touch it.

She was about to take it away when a slow grin tilted up the corners of the man's mouth.

He was handsome wearing a frown; he was devastating with that slow grin that made the little dimple at the corner of his mouth pop.

It was a familiar dimple, and she had the sudden urge to turn on her toes and march right back to her car, drive past the fork in the road, and go somewhere, anywhere, else.

"Carna? Smith's bratty little sister? Man, kid. I wouldn't have recognized your looks, but I suppose you're still just as big of an annoyance now as you used to be."

Maybe he didn't mean to be so insulting; he did seem a little flabbergasted and slightly shocked.

She'd told Smith she wasn't quite sure what day she would arrive since she had to stay at the farm in New Hampshire for an indefinite amount of time, until the new owners had gotten their sea legs.

They were from the city and had never run a farm before.

It had been bittersweet, teaching them to do all the things she knew by heart. Showing them the quirks and foibles of the farm that she loved.

Maybe Smith hadn't told anyone she was coming since her arrival had been so up in the air.

The dimple winked at her, and a memory flashed. It couldn't be.

"Miller?" Smith's best friend from high school, their neighbor, and her nemesis.

His smug look confirmed her guess.

"And you're just as arrogant and conceited as you always were." She grunted. "And just as likely to jump to the absolute wrong conclusion as well."

"You told me the steer opened the chicken coop. Tater Tot, come on." Miller lifted his hands, then slapped them down against his pants. He looked around and then indicated the birds that flapped through the yard. As Carna looked across the wide expanse of grass, two of them hopped up on the porch.

It was cute, but wherever chickens were, they left their markings behind, and nobody wanted that on their porch. Particularly a dude ranch that was trying to impress people from the city, who would never understand that in order to have cute chickens, you had to have the cute chicken coop to go along with it.

"I didn't lie. I never have. I sat in my car and watched that steer use his horn to open the chicken coop. Now whether he did it on purpose or not—"

"I'm sure he did," Miller said, in a condescending tone that made her feel like she was five again. She wanted to stamp her foot. He'd always gotten under her skin. Found a way to tease her and make her so mad she wanted to spit.

Apparently, the dozen or so years since she'd last seen him hadn't changed anything for either one of them.

"Fine. I know it sounds crazy, but it's the truth."

"I'm sure it is, Tater Tot," he said, again using the nickname she'd hated as a child. No one but Miller ever used it, and she'd totally forgot about it.

"Whatever, Ducky Doo Doo," she said derisively, that name she used to call him in return coming easily to her lips. She was ashamed at how easily it came.

His lips twitched in what she almost thought could have been a genuine smile, but he clamped it down immediately.

"Tell me you're just passing through," he said, his hands on his hips, looking at the chickens that happily picked their way through the yard.

"I can tell you that, but it wouldn't be true. And one of us doesn't like to lie, Ducky," she tacked that name on at the end again, just for spite. Or maybe because she wanted to see if she could make him smile again.

No, that couldn't be it at all.

"You're kidding, right? You're just trying to ruin my day."

"You don't have to believe me. But it's the truth."

He took a deep breath, pulling it in through his nose and looking up at the sky like he was pleading with the Almighty for patience.

When he looked back down, his face still seemed tight, like he was not as relaxed as he wanted her to think he was.

"Welcome to Sweet Briar, Tater. You go on up to the house. Darby will be there, and she'll take care of you. Do me a favor, and remind her that I'm working with the more seasoned guests, and I'd like to be stationed as far away from you as possible. Which, I'm sure, suits you as well." His jaw jutted out, and his lips pursed.

"Of course it does, Ducky. I'll be sure to ask Darby to have me working as far away from you as possible. After all, there's a reason you have Do Do in your nickname."

"That happened one time," he said immediately.

"For you. Zero for me. That's one area where I'll admit you have me beat."

She allowed an evil little smile to turn up her lips. She really didn't want to fight with Miller. He seemed like he'd turned into a halfway decent guy. But he hadn't been nice to her, and he was treating her like she hadn't grown up at all.

Surely it was obvious that she had. She'd single-handedly been taking care of her grandparents' farm for the last three years. If there had been a way to save it, she would have found it. She didn't need to be treated like a child who had never set foot on a farm before. And the idea that she would go over and let chickens out on purpose was just ludicrous.

Obviously, Miller hadn't changed at all.

So he deserved to be teased for something that he'd done as a child, since he'd been treating her like a two-year-old since she set foot on the place.

"When you grow up and are able to let it go, let me know, Tater." He started to walk and called over his shoulder, "Pepper, heel." Pepper immediately jumped up, ran to Miller's side, and obediently followed him as he walked away.

Carna let her eyes linger on the broad shoulders for just a moment before she turned away. She didn't need to watch that.

Also, she was a little irrationally irritated at the dog for being so...obedient.

She should have checked with Smith a little more thoroughly about what was going on here before she jumped on the chance to come out. She'd just been happy to have a place to live. She'd sunk every last penny she had into trying to save her grandparents' farm, and she really had no other place to go. This had seemed like a lifesaver at the time, but if she was going to have to be face-to-face with Miller every day, maybe it wasn't going to be as good as what she thought.

Shooting a few quick texts off to Smith – she wouldn't want Miller to get to him first and give him the wrong version of what happened – Carna had a small back-and-forth with him before she shoved her phone back in her pocket. There. Miller could say what he wanted. Smith knew the truth.

Calling Posey, who had been sitting and staring at her the whole time, she walked toward the house.

Posey, shoving her wet nose into Carna's hand, whined, like she was asking Carna to give Miller the benefit of the doubt just to get along.

"No. He's a jerk, and I absolutely do not want to have anything to do with him."

Pick up your copy of *Just a Cowboy's Dream Come True* by Jessie Gussman today!

A Gift from Jessie

View this code through your smart phone camera to be taken to a page where you can download a FREE ebook when you sign up to get updates from Jessie Gussman! Find out why people say, "Jessie's is the only newsletter I open and read" and "You make my day brighter. Love, love, love reading your newsletters. I don't know where you find time to write books. You are so busy living life. A true blessing." and "I know from now on that I can't be drinking my morning coffee while reading your newsletter – I laughed so hard I sprayed it out all over the table!"

Claim your free book from Jessie!

Escape to more faith-filled romance series by Jessie Gussman!

The Complete Sweet Water, North Dakota Reading Order:

Series One: Sweet Water Ranch Western Cowboy Romance (11 book series)

Series Two: Coming Home to North Dakota (12 book series)

Series Three: Flyboys of Sweet Briar Ranch in North Dakota (13 book series)

Series Four: Sweet View Ranch Western Cowboy Romance (10 book series)

Spinoffs and More! Additional Series You'll Love:

Jessie's First Series: Sweet Haven Farm (4 book series)

Small-Town Romance: The Baxter Boys (5 book series)

Bad-Boy Sweet Romance: Richmond Rebels Sweet Romance (3 book series)

Sweet Water Spinoff: Cowboy Crossing (9 book series)

Holiday Romance: Cowboy Mountain Christmas (6 book series)

Small Town Romantic Comedy: Good Grief, Idaho (5 book series)

True Stories from Jessie's Farm: Stories from Jessie Gussman's Newsletter (3 book series)

Reader-Favorite! Sweet Beach Romance: Blueberry Beach (8 book series)

Cowboy Mountain Christmas Spinoff: A Heartland Cowboy Christmas (9 book series)

Blueberry Beach Spinoff: Strawberry Sands (10 book series)

Printed in the USA
CPSIA information can be obtained
at www.ICGtesting.com
LVHW022142180524
780462LV00013B/804

9 781953 066855